The wind in her ears kept Elizabeth from hearing the Jeep until it had pulled up right alongside her. It was Ryan.

"What are you doing out here?" he shouted over the combined noises of the wind, the engine, and the crashing surf.

Elizabeth shrugged, trying to clear her head. "Thinking," she answered. She didn't have to say about what—from the set of his jaw she saw that he already knew.

"Yeah. Well, sometimes it's not a good idea to think too much."

"Ryan . . ." Elizabeth began, putting one hand over his on the stick shift. Immediately, reflexively, their fingers twined together. Elizabeth felt the same jolt of electricity she'd experienced the night they'd kissed as they squeezed each other's fingers hard. Then, just as suddenly, he dropped her hand.

"This is a bad idea," he said, his voice raw. "I thought you understood that."

"Maybe I do," Elizabeth admitted, "but I'd like to talk about it."

Ryan looked at her, then quickly looked away.

"I wouldn't," he said flatly.

SWEET VALLEY UNIVERSITY®

Elizabeth's Summer Love

Written by
Laurie John

Created by
FRANCINE PASCAL

BANTAM BOOKS
NEW YORK · TORONTO · LONDON · SYDNEY · AUCKLAND

RL 6, age 12 and up

ELIZABETH'S SUMMER LOVE
A Bantam Book / July 1996

Sweet Valley High® and Sweet Valley University®
are registered trademarks of Francine Pascal
Conceived by Francine Pascal
Produced by Daniel Weiss Associates, Inc.
33 West 17th Street
New York, NY 10011

ISBN: 0-553-56705-5

Published simultaneously in the United States and Canada

Bantam Books are published by Bantam Books, a division of Bantam
Doubleday Dell Publishing Group, Inc. Its trademark, consisting of the
words "Bantam Books" and the portrayal of a rooster, is Registered in
U.S. Patent and Trademark Office and in other countries. Marca
Registrada. Bantam Books, 1540 Broadway, New York, New York 10036.

PRINTED IN THE UNITED STATES OF AMERICA

OPM   0 9 8 7 6 5 4 3 2 1

To Courtney Brooke Weisman

Chapter One

Jessica Wakefield awoke with a groan, slamming her hand down hard on the buzzing alarm clock. She had only been a lifeguard for a month, and she was already starting to hate it. It had all seemed so glamorous when Nina Harper first suggested it—Jessica had instantly pictured herself running around in a sleek, sexy suit, rescuing adoring, gorgeous guys. But now she knew the truth: being a lifeguard was plain hard work. She hadn't rescued a single cute guy yet. As for glamorous, it seemed as if she spent most of the day passing out Band-Aids, picking up glass in the sand, and banning dogs from the beach.

Jessica held herself motionless in her single bed, listening for signs of life from her housemates at Sweet Valley Shore. The three-story Victorian beach house they'd rented had six bedrooms. Jessica and Wendy Wolman had the two attic

1

rooms on the top floor, Jessica's identical twin Elizabeth's room was on the second floor with Nina's, and Ben Mercer and Winston Egbert slept on the ground floor.

Wendy and Nina were the only returning lifeguards. Nina's boyfriend, Bryan Nelson, had originally planned to come as well, but he'd found an old high school friend, Ben, to take over his bedroom at the last minute when he'd been offered a job in Washington, D.C., instead. Wendy was nice enough—a little plain and boring—but Ben was a royal pain in the butt, and his ex-girlfriend Rachel Max was even worse. Rachel was head lifeguard of the rival South Beach Squad, and she was rude, nasty, and just all-around unbearable. Jessica couldn't even *stand* Ben, but that didn't seem to matter to Rachel, who acted like a jealous psycho every chance she got. Was it *Jessica's* fault if Ben followed her around like a stray dog?

Jessica sighed out loud. She wished that handsome, elusive Ryan Taylor, leader of the Sweet Valley Shore Lifeguard Squad, was living with them instead of Ben. She closed her eyes again, picturing Ryan's tall, muscular frame, his guarded, gold-flecked brown eyes, and the sun-bleached highlights in his cropped, curly brown hair. Now *Ryan* was the kind of guy a girl could get out of bed for in the morning. Unfortunately, thinking of her boss reminded Jessica that she was supposed to be getting up for work, not for fun.

And Ryan was *definitely* no fun at work.

Maybe I should call in sick, Jessica thought in a flash of inspiration. Even as she thought it, though, she knew it was impossible—she'd called in sick once a week, every week, for the last month. And to top things off, this morning was Saturday of the three-day Fourth of July weekend. Even though the Fourth wasn't actually until Monday, the lifeguards had been thoroughly briefed on what they could expect during all three days of this Mother of All California Beach Holidays: total pandemonium.

Great, Jessica thought, wishing she could pull the soft white comforter over her head and go back to sleep. And it wasn't just that lifeguarding wasn't turning out the way she'd planned, either—it was awful working with Elizabeth and Ryan every day. It was hard to believe that Elizabeth, Little Miss Perfect, would actually play around on her boyfriend, Tom Watts, but hadn't Jessica seen Elizabeth and Ryan kissing with her own eyes only a month before? Jessica hadn't managed to catch them at anything that overt since then, but every time the two of them even walked into the same room, you could practically feel the temperature shoot up five degrees. What made it doubly galling was that Elizabeth was cheating with Ryan, the guy that *Jessica* wanted.

It was actually kind of bizarre. Even though Jessica and Elizabeth looked identical, they had always had very different personalities. Elizabeth was studious, responsible, levelheaded—totally into her classes, her causes, and her boyfriend. Jessica, on the other hand, was the fun, single one—the one used to grabbing a guy's attention. Sometimes at a party, when Jessica pulled out all the stops, the men practically stampeded over Elizabeth to get to her. So why did Ryan prefer Elizabeth? It was totally inexplicable.

Slipping her bare feet reluctantly out of bed and onto the cold wood floor, Jessica walked silently to the window and peered down at the beach outside from between the mini-blinds. Unbelievable! The weather was atrocious. She was used to a little fog in the mornings, but nothing like this. The whole sky was an ugly, steely gray—it looked like it could actually rain.

That's it, she told herself, making up her mind. *No one appreciates me anyway. They'll have to get along without me today.* Throwing a thick burgundy robe on over her thin white negligee, Jessica opened her bedroom door and padded barefoot down the stairs to Nina's room.

"Nina!" Jessica whispered, knocking gently. "You awake?"

"What do you want?" Nina grumbled back. It was obvious from the sleep in her voice that Jessica had just woken her.

Jessica opened her housemate's door and stepped inside. The room was dark, but Jessica

4

could easily make out Nina's beaded black braids against the bright yellow of her pillowcase. Nina's face was turned toward the wall as if she hoped that ignoring Jessica might make her go away.

"I feel really sick," Jessica whispered, keeping her voice low so the rest of the house wouldn't hear her. "I know this is your day off, but could you take my shift, Nina? Please?"

Nina heaved a long-suffering sigh and rolled to face her best friend's sister. "You're sick all the time," Nina said. "And anyway, you look fine to me. Go to work."

"Please, Nina," Jessica begged. "I know I don't *look* that bad, but I really am coming down with some kind of flu or something. I feel awful. Here," she offered, "feel how hot my forehead is." Jessica knelt next to Nina's bed, placing her own golden tan hand against her perfectly fine forehead.

"No, thanks," Nina declined, turning back to the wall.

Jessica smiled slyly to herself—she had guessed that Nina wouldn't actually check her on that.

"I'd hate to think that someone might get hurt, or even worse, because I was too sick to do the kind of job you always do, Nina," Jessica gushed, a practiced quiver in her voice. She knew from experience that Nina wasn't easily swayed by flattery, but she also knew that Nina took life-guarding very seriously—she was assistant head lifeguard of the Sweet Valley Shore Squad. Nina wouldn't dare take a chance where lives were at stake. Of course, Jessica was also counting on the fact that Nina hadn't seen the weather yet.

"All right. I'll take your shift," Nina groaned, right on cue. "But this is absolutely the last time! I mean it."

"You're the best," Jessica whispered, backing quickly out of Nina's room and closing the door behind her. She could practically hear her cozy, still warm bed calling her as she slipped silently up the stairs, thoroughly pleased with her acting job.

What a sucker! Jessica gloated to herself as she snuggled back under the covers. *Now if only I could figure out how to do this every day. . . .*

"I can't believe this," Nina muttered as she scanned the almost totally empty beach from her position at the Main Tower railing. She was wearing her red lifeguard bathing suit, but she'd had to put her heavy orange lifeguard jacket and navy blue sweatpants on over it. "Have you ever seen such horrible weather on a Fourth of July weekend in your *life?*" she demanded of Ryan, who was standing next to her. He was watching the surf through binoculars.

Ryan shook his head, his brown eyes clearly worried.

"I don't think I've ever seen weather this bad in July, period," he responded. "It's not normal."

Nina nodded. The sky was so dark, it almost didn't seem like daytime, and she was sure it was going to start raining any minute. Even with the binoculars she could barely make out the South Tower at the far end of the beach, where Elizabeth was working with Wendy.

"If this doesn't clear up, it'll kill the whole weekend," Nina observed.

"You're not kidding," Ryan responded. "The stores on the boardwalk plan for the Fourth all year. If things don't turn around, they're going to lose tons of money."

Nina nodded, knowing how dependent the beach merchants were on holiday tourists.

"I'm going downstairs to get the weather radio," Ryan decided. "You're on watch."

Nina acknowledged his order by resuming her scan of the beach as Ryan took off. Since he lived in a room at the base of the tower, Ryan sometimes took the radio there at night to listen to the weather reports for the next day. Nina knew that no one had predicted this storm—she kept a weather radio in her room too. Every good lifeguard made it her business to stay on top of the weather forecast. In an ocean emergency the weather could literally make the difference between life and death.

Nina watched for a while as a teenage boy rode a body board near the shoreline in front of the tower. The water looked wicked—ugly, gray, and choppy—and the kid apparently had the good sense not to go out too far. Still, there were several major riptides working in the area, and Nina was keeping an eye on him.

She knew she should concentrate more fully on her job, but there was so little happening on the beach that she couldn't help letting her mind wander a bit. There was going to be a rave in the abandoned cannery warehouse on Sunday night— it was supposed to be a big secret, but the whole town knew about it—and on Monday there was a free concert and fireworks. A lot of people would come to the beach on both those days and stay into the night. If it was hot, there'd be plenty of drinking going on, and drinking in the sun would lead to accidents and fights later on—especially when some of the drunks started their drinking at ten in the morning. The Sweet Valley Shore life-guards always racked up more saves and incident reports on the Fourth of July than on any other day of the year, although Labor Day was usually a close second place.

"I found it," Ryan announced, coming back to the railing, radio in hand, "and it sounds totally grim. That hurricane in Baja took an unexpected left. They're predicting high winds and rain all day—even a chance of lightning."

"Lightning!" Nina exclaimed. "Here? That's impossible."

"I've seen it once," Ryan conceded. "But not in July."

"Too weird," Nina replied.

"Yeah," he agreed. "Well, I'm going to close the beach. It's practically empty anyway, and there's no sense in everyone standing out here in towers if there's going to be lightning. You go tell the others to take off and I'll close up."

"Wow," Nina said, awed. She had never seen the beach closed before. All last summer they hadn't closed a single day. "Do you want some help closing up?" Nina tried to remember what it said in the lifeguarding manual about closing the beach. "Aren't we supposed to put up No Swimming signs or something?"

"I'll do all that," Ryan told her. He raised his whistle to his lips and signaled the kid on the body board out of the water. "You go on and tell the others," he directed.

The Mighty Immortal Something or Others were kicking the stuffing out of the evil alien from Planet Ooze, but Winston wasn't paying attention. Normally he enjoyed a cartoon or two in the morning, but not all day every day. He sighed, wishing that Wendy were around to entertain him—they'd become close over the past few weeks—but she was working at the beach. Part of Winston still couldn't believe he hadn't made the lifeguard squad, and part of him couldn't believe he'd been dumb enough to think he would. He'd never been the jock type—he must have been nuts!

It would have been fun, though. Not to mention that he desperately needed the money. The gold bracelet he'd given his girlfriend, Denise Waters, before she'd gone off to Europe for the summer had seriously depleted his savings, and paying Nina for his share of the security deposit and first month's rent on the beach house had left him totally bankrupt.

Winston knew that his continued unemployed status was becoming a household joke, but what could he do? For a while after the lifeguard tryouts Winston had hoped that he could convince Ryan to hire him after all. Every day he'd gone to the beach in front of the Main Tower and run wind sprints, swum pretend races to the buoys, cautioned children who were perfectly safe, and done everything else he could think of to convince Ryan what a great addition to the squad he'd make. But it hadn't worked. In fact, it *more* than hadn't worked.

Winston would have thought, considering how long he'd known the Wakefield twins, that Jessica or Elizabeth could have told him. But they hadn't. They'd left that little job for Wendy.

"Winnie," she'd said one afternoon while he was resting on the sofa after a particularly grueling workout, "you've got to give this up."

"Give what up?" he'd asked innocently. He'd looked up from flexing what he'd dared to hope was a growing right biceps to see Wendy standing over him in her red lifeguard suit, still salty from the beach. He remembered noticing how tan she was getting.

"This running around at the beach. Pretending you're on the squad," she'd said.

"I'm not *pretending* I'm on the squad," he'd informed her stuffily. "I'm auditioning for it." He'd lifted the waistband of his bright orange swimming trunks just enough to check his own tan line—nothing.

She'd hesitated, then plopped down beside him on the couch. "The thing is," she'd continued, incredibly kindly, "lifeguard auditions are over."

"But they could still—"

"No," she'd interrupted. "They already have a couple of alternates in mind in case they need anyone else. Besides . . ." She'd trailed off uncomfortably, her clear gray eyes suddenly refusing to meet his.

"What?"

She'd shaken her head. "Nothing," she'd said.

"What?" he'd demanded.

"It's just that some of the people on the squad, well, Marcus and Paula . . . they're laughing at you."

"*Laughing* at me!" Winston had responded, stunned. He'd thought he was really coming along. He hardly ever tripped in the sand more than once a sprint by then, and that pink plastic gadget he'd found to pinch his nostrils shut had shaved nearly a second off his swimming time.

"They're laughing at me?" he'd repeated.

"Not to be mean!" Wendy had assured him. "Everyone on the squad really likes you, Winnie. It's just . . . well . . . you're not really lifeguard material."

"No," he'd said numbly. Of course he wasn't. How could he have made such a fool of himself? It had been humiliating.

"There are still lots of stores hiring on the boardwalk," Wendy had suggested encouragingly, smiling.

Winston sighed loudly to himself and buried his head under a striped sofa cushion as he relived his epic failure. The only good thing to come out of this summer so far was his friendship with Wendy.

The phone in the kitchen rang loudly, interrupting his thoughts. Winston jumped, then ran to answer it. Maybe it was Denise calling to say how much she missed him! Better still, maybe it was Ryan calling to say that they'd reconsidered and they needed Winston on the squad after all. Maybe . . .

"Hello?" he blurted, snatching up the receiver.

Maybe it was Isabella Ricci calling for Jessica.

"I've *got* it, Winston," Jessica informed him haughtily from the upstairs extension.

"You're kidding, right?" Isabella said skeptically. Jessica knew that tone so well, she could practically *hear* Isabella raise those perfectly arched dark eyebrows.

"I know it sounds crazy, Izzy," Jessica insisted, "but you have to see them together."

Jessica had just told Isabella about Elizabeth and Ryan. She sat up on her bed and pushed away the fashion magazine she'd been reading. Wendy's dog, Paloma Perro, unhappy with the lack of room afforded by the new arrangement, jumped off the bed and forced his way through the just barely open crack of Jessica's door and into the hall. *He's getting fat,* Jessica realized as she watched the mutt struggle out. *Maybe I should quit feeding him so many treats on the sly.*

"I just can't believe Elizabeth would do something like that," Isabella repeated. "Cheat on Tom? For a summer fling?"

"Well, of course she denies it," Jessica admitted. "But every time they get together, there's so much tension in the air you could cut it with a chain saw. And Ryan totally favors her—gives her all the good shifts and assignments and barely even notices anyone else on the squad."

"Anyone like you, for example?" Isabella asked perceptively.

Jessica was glad that her best friend couldn't see her flushing face. "No," she lied. "That's not it. I mean, sure, I'd like a chance at the guy—who wouldn't? But that's not the point. I just don't think it's right."

13

"And *I* don't think it's happening," Isabella said dismissively. "You said yourself that you don't have any proof."

"Only the fact that I caught them kissing," Jessica reminded her.

"A month ago," Isabella countered. "Everyone makes mistakes sometime, but you know Liz isn't a liar, Jess. If she says nothing's going on now, I think you should believe her."

Jessica had somehow forgotten how tolerant Isabella was. Obviously she wasn't going to get any sympathy from *her*.

"Anyway," Isabella said, changing the subject. "Elizabeth is *not* the reason I called. I want to come down and stay with you this weekend . . . spend the Fourth at the beach."

"You do?" Jessica asked excitedly. "Izzy, how great!"

It would be fun to see her friend. They could go shopping and to the rave and . . . "But how come you're not spending the long weekend with Danny?" Jessica asked as the obvious finally occurred to her.

"I was going to," Isabella admitted, "but Tom's taking the weekend off from his communications course and driving down from Colorado to see Danny—I'd just be a third wheel. And besides, the Fourth of July isn't any fun unless you're at the beach."

"You are so right," Jessica agreed, her brain

14

kicking into high gear as the seeds of a new plan sprouted. "It *is* more fun at the beach. We're all having such a great time here," she lied.

No need to mention the fact that her housemates were getting on her nerves or that the weather totally stunk and showed no signs of improving.

"Hey, *I've* got an idea!" Jessica added, hoping she sounded spontaneous. "Why don't all *three* of you come down? That way you'll get to have some time alone with Danny, and Tom can see Elizabeth. It'll be a great surprise for her!"

"Why would you want Tom to come down if you honestly believe there's something going on between Elizabeth and that lifeguard?" Isabella asked suspiciously.

But Jessica was way ahead of her.

"You know," she answered smoothly, "you were so right about that after all. I should give my sister more credit. Of *course* Elizabeth wouldn't cheat on Tom. What was I thinking?"

"I don't know," Isabella said, "but I don't think bringing the guys is such a good idea anyway. Elizabeth isn't going to have any time to spend with Tom if she has to work all weekend."

"You *have* to bring Danny and Tom," Jessica urged. "Liz will be devastated if she finds out that her boyfriend was so close and didn't come to see her."

She might have put a *little* too much emphasis on "boyfriend," but Jessica rushed ahead anyway.

"Besides, there's a huge rave tomorrow, and Elizabeth won't have a date if Tom doesn't come. They can spend time together at the party."

"Okay." Isabella gave in. "I'll ask the guys if they want to come. If they do, we'll drive out tomorrow morning and leave after the fireworks on Monday."

Jessica was exhilarated as she hung up the phone. This was the break she'd been waiting for! Elizabeth was going to have to spend the whole weekend with Tom now, and when Ryan saw them together, maybe he would *finally* get the picture that Elizabeth was not available. Jessica, on the other hand, was completely available. Not to mention sexier, more fun, and just generally more Ryan's type. Maybe Elizabeth didn't see it, but Jessica did—there was a lot more to Ryan than he wanted people to know. And Jessica couldn't wait to learn every single secret.

"Still watching cartoons?" Jessica asked Winston in that extremely superior voice she put on whenever she was about to make some major conquest. He'd known her too long not to recognize it.

"For your information," Winston replied, assuming an equally haughty tone, "the Muppets are not animated. Ergo, their show is not a cartoon."

He looked up from where he'd practically grown into oneness with the sofa as Jessica crossed the living room. She was wearing a sheer white blouse with tight black jeans, and her long blond hair was pulled back into a sleek ponytail.

"Hey! What are you all dressed up for?" he asked, surprised back into his normal voice. He felt suddenly self-conscious in the outfit that was becoming his daily uniform—ratty gray sweatpants and an equally ratty blue sweatshirt. He tried to remember if he had brushed his hair, but he couldn't. He *knew* he hadn't brushed his teeth.

"For *your* information," Jessica answered him, "there is a very major party tomorrow. *Ergo,* I need a manicure."

"I thought you said you weren't going because you didn't have a date," he protested.

"Things change, Winston," Jessica said mysteriously, looking very pleased with herself.

Winston sighed, knowing that look too well. In combination with the voice there was no room for doubt—she was up to something again.

"I'll need a new outfit, too," she announced, more to herself than to him as she headed for the door.

"But I thought you were supposed to be . . . ," Winston began as Jessica grabbed her coat off the rack and opened the front door. Just then a surprisingly sudden, vicious gust of wind tore the door from her hands and slammed it shut behind her.

"Sick," he finished, addressing an empty room.

Chapter Two

Nina ducked her head against the growing storm as she walked along the deserted boardwalk into town. She had intended to take advantage of her early dismissal from the beach to buy some stamps at the post office, but now she wished she'd gone straight home. The weather was bizarre—there was no other word for it. The wind that had come up over the last hour was incredibly strong, and she hoped the local windsurfers would obey the No Swimming signs Ryan had posted. There was no way a beginner would even be able to stand up in these conditions, but Nina had seen experienced windsurfers go out in howling winds before.

"Nina. Nina!"

Nina could barely distinguish her name over the roar of the wind, but someone was definitely calling her. She squinted down the empty boardwalk.

"Hey! Over here!" Paul Jackson called from the doorway of the surfboard rental shop. He motioned her over, and Nina was happy for the excuse to get out of the wind as she ducked inside his shop.

"Crazy weather," he observed, grinning as she slipped gratefully through the door and unzipped her heavy lifeguard jacket.

"I can't believe it," she agreed, looking around. The tiny store was totally empty except for her, Paul, and rack after rack of rental boards. On a normal, sunny Saturday those racks would be nearly empty by now. "Renting a lot of surfboards today?" she teased.

"Oh, yeah," Paul said sarcastically, cranking up the grin into that killer smile of his. As usual he looked incredibly handsome and preppy in a red polo shirt with blue canvas slacks.

Nina wished he wouldn't smile at her like that. Every time he did, she got so hopelessly confused. She was *totally* in love with her boyfriend, Bryan. So why was it that every time Paul smiled, she immediately forgot all about Bryan? She jumped guiltily as she remembered that the reason she'd come to town in the first place was to buy stamps to mail Bryan a letter.

It's his own fault, she thought suddenly, surprising herself. *If Bryan had come to the shore like he was supposed to instead of taking that job on Capitol Hill, I wouldn't even be here with Paul right now!*

19

Still, there was no denying the fact that she felt guilty. Nina weakly returned Paul's smile, trying to regain control.

"If you want to sell some of those boards at the end of the summer, I might want to buy one," she offered. "*If* the price is right."

Paul smiled again. Nina flinched.

"Actually," he said, "they're all for sale right now. See anything you like?"

"You're kidding." Nina looked around in amazement. "They're not really for sale yet, are they?"

"In this business you turn over the stock as fast as you can," Paul informed her. "If someone wants to buy a board, you sell it while it's still worth something, because by the end of the summer it may be trash."

"I see your point," Nina said, remembering some of the spectacular collisions she had witnessed from the tower. People who rented surfboards tended to have no idea how to actually use them.

"Come on, take a look," Paul urged, gesturing toward the racks behind him. "How much do you weigh?"

"Excuse me?" Nina returned, shocked. It wasn't that she was *ashamed* of her weight, but she'd always been a little sensitive about it. She was usually very careful about what she ate, and she knew she was in terrific shape or she wouldn't have made the lifeguard squad. Still, some things were better left on a need-to-know basis. She could feel a hot, embarrassed blush spreading across her dark cheeks.

But Paul just laughed. "I had a feeling you were going to react like that," he said. "You've never bought a surfboard before, have you?"

"No," Nina admitted. "I've only surfed a few times."

"Well, asking the customer's weight is a pretty common practice," Paul explained. "Any good salesperson will at least try to guess it before they suggest a board."

"Oh," Nina said, worried now that she had overreacted. She still wasn't planning to volunteer that particular piece of information, though.

"You don't even have to tell me." Paul looked Nina up and down and guessed a five-pound range that was exactly on target. "Inexperienced, but strong. Coordinated. Used to the water."

He walked to a rack near the center of the store and pulled out a mid-size board from somewhere near the bottom.

"This one might be perfect for you," he said. "It's a six-eight, which is more board than you really need for your size, but it'll be easier to learn on. You can go shorter later, when you know what you're doing."

Nina looked at the board Paul had selected and loved it instantly. It was white, with narrow turquoise stripes on either side of the center stringer and three small turquoise fins to match.

"This is a pintail thruster," Paul told her, indicating the three fins and pointed tail end that gave the board its name. "It's a very basic board," he continued. "Perfect for a beginner."

"It's nice," she said noncommittally, looking it over, getting ready to bargain.

"I chose it because it's only been out a few times," Paul confided. "There's not a ding on it." He turned that distracting smile her way, and she noticed once again how flawless his light brown skin was. If she wasn't already dating Bryan . . .

"How much is it?" Nina blurted, forgetting to act cool. Her heart was pounding like crazy. *This is ridiculous,* she scolded herself.

"For *you,* special deal. It's on the house."

"Paul!" she protested. "You can't just give away surfboards. This isn't even your shop!"

"Don't worry." He grinned. "I'll pay for it. Think of it as a gift from a friend."

But Nina wasn't sure she wanted him to be that kind of friend. Even slightly used, the board was worth a couple hundred dollars.

"Thanks, but I'll pay for it myself," she told him.

"Nina . . . ," he began.

"I'll give you a hundred for it," she offered, expecting him to counter.

"Oh, all right," he agreed, heaving a theatrical sigh. "If you insist."

"All right?" she squeaked. "Paul! That's not enough!"

"Who's the salesman here?" He laughed. "You're supposed to be trying to wheedle me *down,* not up."

"I can't buy it unless you charge me something fair," she insisted.

They finally agreed on a hundred and fifty dollars, which Nina thought was still way too low, but Paul insisted was perfectly reasonable.

"If you were a tourist, I might have charged you a little more," he admitted, "but think of it as your lifeguard's discount. Hal won't mind," he assured her, referring to the store's owner. "And besides, this is my last day in the shop."

"What!" Nina exclaimed, not liking how concerned she sounded. "Where are you going?" she asked, more casually.

"I'm joining the South Beach Squad," Paul said. "One of their guys is out with the measles, and they need someone experienced to replace him."

In a way it was almost a relief. The Sweet Valley Shore Squad was so competitive with the South Beach Squad that practically the only time they ever spoke to each other was to exchange insults. Professional pride had something to do with it, but the cash bonus the town gave the squad with the best record at the end of the summer was no doubt the biggest part of the animosity between the two groups. Sometimes Nina wished that they would eliminate the merit-pay bonus altogether, so that people could concentrate on their jobs instead of obsessing over daily tallies of saves and incidents. On the other hand, it *would* be nice to earn the extra money, and so far the squads were pretty even. . . .

"Does this mean we can't be friends anymore?" Nina teased, feeling more at ease now that Paul was about to be safely out of reach.

"Not at all," he said, leaning in so close that if she'd puckered her lips, they would have touched his. "In fact, I was hoping you'd go to the rave with me tomorrow."

"Is it hot in here, or is it you?" Nina blurted, stepping back and waving one hand frantically in front of her face. "I mean, *me!* Is it *me?*"

She was getting in deeper by the minute.

"It's *extremely* hot in here," Paul agreed, letting his dark chocolate eyes skim her body. "And I'm pretty sure it *is* you." He started to reach for her waist.

For a second, she almost let him. Paul had taken her by surprise and kissed her once before, at the Memorial Day bonfire. But that time had been an accident—she truly hadn't expected it. If she let him do it again, there would be no excuse.

"Paul," she objected, stopping his hands with her own. "I have a boyfriend, remember?"

At first she thought he was going to go for it

anyway, but finally he took his hands away.

"How could I forget?" he asked lightly. "You remind me every day."

"Maybe you should ask yourself why I feel the need to do that," Nina told him stiffly.

"Maybe *you* should ask *yourself* why," Paul replied. "Have you ever heard of protesting too much?"

"Have *you* ever heard of pushing too hard?" she countered, becoming a little angry.

He laughed. "All right. It's a standoff. But you *will* go to the rave with me, right?"

"You're impossible," she said, smiling in spite of herself.

"I'll take that as a yes," he decided, reaching for her again.

Nina knew she should move away as Paul's strong hands closed around her waist. But she didn't. Almost without conscious consent, her own arms came up and circled his body. Nina heard him catch his breath as he pulled her closer and she gripped him more tightly.

And that was when she felt it. The hard, unexpected object near the small of his back. Something wasn't right.

"What *is* that?" she asked, pulling back.

"What's what?" He smiled, trying to hold on. But Nina stepped quickly away.

"That thing on your back," she insisted. "What is it?"

"Oh," Paul said, looking sheepish. "*That*. It's nothing."

He yanked his red shirt up from the waistband of his pants and reached around behind him. "See?" he said, holding up a long, jagged knife by its molded ebony handle.

Nina gasped involuntarily as she took in the highly polished steel of the razor-sharp blade. Ryan had warned her there was something suspicious about Paul. Trying to maintain a calm outward appearance, Nina nervously gauged the distance between herself and the door.

Paul read her expression easily and laughed.

"Relax," he told her, slipping the blade back into the sheath on his belt. "It's just my diving knife. My dad gave it to me for Christmas, and he was so proud of himself for thinking of it that I didn't have the heart to tell him it was major overkill. I was planning to go diving after work today, but this weather took care of that idea. Visibility is zero."

Nina felt a flood of relief, followed quickly by embarrassment. For a second there she'd almost been afraid of him.

You still should be, she told herself harshly, remembering how close she'd just come to kissing him.

Elizabeth Wakefield walked alone along the edge of the foaming surf, enjoying the way the wind whipped her long blond ponytail behind her. It would be a nightmare to comb out later, but the walk was just what she needed now. The situation with Ryan was getting too hot to handle, and the cold salt air provided some welcome relief—almost as if it could cool her overheated brain.

Ever since the night that Jessica had caught them kissing in Ryan's room at the tower, Elizabeth and Ryan had kept a safe distance from each other. They worked together a lot, of course, but never alone—and they'd never discussed what had taken place between them that night. Their separation had just kind of happened, silently imposed by each.

For her own part Elizabeth still burned with shame whenever she remembered the way she had thrown herself into Ryan's arms, totally forgetting Tom. She couldn't believe she was capable of such a major betrayal of trust, but every time she got anywhere near Ryan, she wanted to do it again. Elizabeth wasn't sure what Ryan was afraid of, but it did make him look pretty unprofessional to be carrying on with a member of his own squad. *Maybe that's it,* she told herself. Ryan took lifeguarding so seriously, it was like some kind of holy mission for him.

The wind in her ears kept Elizabeth from hearing the Jeep until it had pulled up right alongside her. It was Ryan. They were dressed alike in their lifeguard-issue orange jackets and navy blue sweatpants, but Ryan's jacket was unzipped, revealing his deeply tanned chest and washboard stomach. Elizabeth looked away too late—she was already mentally exploring that expanse of smooth, bare skin.

"What are you doing out here?" Ryan shouted over the combined noises of the wind, the engine, and the crashing surf.

Elizabeth shrugged, trying to clear her head. "Thinking," she answered. She didn't have to say about what—from the set of his jaw she saw that he already knew.

"Yeah. Well," he said, looking down and fiddling with the gearshift. "Sometimes it's not a good idea to think too much."

"Maybe," Elizabeth agreed, picking up his meaning. "And maybe sometimes thinking is all you *can* do."

It seemed to Elizabeth that Ryan looked relieved as the message behind her words sank in.

"I was going to make the rounds." He indicated the open beach in front of them with a nod. "I've got No Swimming signs up everywhere, but you never know if some genius is going to decide to go in anyway. Want to come?"

"Sure," she agreed, climbing in on the passenger side.

Just be normal, Elizabeth instructed herself as they drove slowly down the beach. *Act normal.* But the silence between them was stifling. She had to break it.

"This is quite a storm," she volunteered at last, trying to overcome the awkwardness. "I've lived in California my whole life and I've *never* seen weather like this."

"That seems to be the general consensus," Ryan replied shortly.

So much for chatting about the weather. Elizabeth tried desperately to think of another safe subject to kill time with, but she couldn't come up with anything. All she could think about was him. And her. And him with her. . . .

"What are you wearing sunglasses for?" she asked finally. "It's practically dark already."

"The sand," Ryan explained, taking his left hand off the steering wheel to gesture at the blowing sand outside the Jeep. "It hurts like crazy when it gets underneath my contacts."

Elizabeth hadn't known he wore contacts. *Then again,* she told herself, *you don't know much about Ryan.* But she wanted to—more than anything. They had to talk.

"Ryan . . . ," Elizabeth began, putting one hand over his on the stick shift. Immediately, reflexively, their fingers twined together. Elizabeth felt the same jolt of electricity she'd experienced the night they'd kissed as they squeezed each other's fingers hard. Then, just as suddenly, he dropped her hand.

"This is a bad idea," he said, his voice raw. "I thought you understood that."

"Maybe I do," Elizabeth admitted, "but I'd like to talk about it."

Ryan looked at her, then quickly looked away.

"I wouldn't," he said flatly.

"I can't believe you're still wearing those ratty old sweatpants," Wendy complained to Winston. "Don't you sleep in those?"

"So what?" he defended himself. "They're multipurpose."

"So *what?*" she came back. "They're pajamas."

"I know," Winston admitted, scraping the last bit of ice cream from the pint in his hand and licking the plastic spoon. He looked miserable, actually. His chestnut curls were mashed flat against the back of his head, as if he hadn't combed them all day, and his freckled face needed a shave.

They were sitting at the kitchen table, eating their favorite snack—a pint each of the handmade, super-rich ice cream from Udder Delights, the local ice-cream parlor. Paloma Perro was on the floor at their side, polishing off a pint of his own personal favorite—Cookies and Berries.

"Your dog's getting fat," Winston observed. Wendy recognized a feeble attempt to change the subject when she heard one, but she rushed to her pet's defense anyway.

"He is not!" she objected. "He's just filling out."

"Yeah," Winston agreed. "*Way* out. Face it, Wendy—he's turning into the world's shaggiest pig."

Now that Winston mentioned it, Paloma did seem a little . . . well . . . chubby.

"I don't understand it," Wendy said, genuinely puzzled. "I don't feed him that much."

"You call buying him his own pint of ice cream every day 'not that much'?" Winston wanted to know.

"Not every day—only two or three times a week," Wendy corrected him. "And the rest of the time I'm very strict. I never feed him treats or table scraps or *anything*. You'd think that with all the exercise he does, he'd be able to work off a little ice cream."

"All the *exercise* he does?" Winston howled, laughing harder than he had for days. "If that dog had fingers, he'd ask for his own remote!"

"Well, you would know," Wendy countered, smiling in spite of herself. "You're our resident authority on couch potatoes these days."

"I prefer 'couch commando,'" Winston informed her, grinning back good-naturedly.

Wendy was glad she'd made such a fast friend in Winston. They had a lot in common, really. Neither one of them was especially good looking, and they'd both always compensated for it by being funny instead. But where Winston's clowning had gotten him accepted into the coolest group at his high school and made him popular at college too, Wendy had always remained on the fringes.

Sometimes she thought it was easier for guys than for girls. If a guy was incredibly funny, like Winston, or if he was a really good athlete or musician or something, it didn't matter so much what he looked like. With girls, on the other hand, it seemed that if you didn't measure up to some minimum standard of beauty, no one cared what else you had to offer. All Wendy's life people had described her as having "a good personality." A good personality—the social kiss of death.

Suddenly the hair along Paloma's neck stood up and he growled ominously.

"See?" Wendy giggled, resuming her conversation with Winston. "Now you've insulted him."

"No, I think someone might have knocked at the door," Winston said, craning his neck to listen.

"It was only the wind," Wendy suggested.

The doorbell rang and Paloma ran off, barking in a fit of vindication.

"Or it *could* be someone at the door," Wendy amended, getting up to answer it.

The minute Wendy saw who was standing on the doorstep, she knew that she and Winston were about to have a serious fight. The poor, wind-blown kid outside had been showing up so frequently lately that Wendy felt she should invite him in for coffee or something. He stood clutching his unwelcome package tightly against his rumpled white shirt, his green florist's apron whipping out behind him.

"Hi, Bob," she said unhappily, reaching for his delivery clipboard.

"How's it going?" he returned, pointing to where he wanted her to sign.

Wendy signed on the line reluctantly and took possession of the long gold box of roses as if it were a pipe bomb. She didn't even have to look at the card—she knew who they were from.

Pedro Paloma. He'd sent her flowers at least once every week since their disastrous date a month before. The date that Wendy's *good friend* Winston had blackmailed Pedro into taking her on. Wendy had been so psyched that her favorite singer, a *celebrity*, would want to go out with her. It had all seemed too good to be true. And it was. Every time the flowers showed up, Wendy got furious with Winston all over again. *How dare he put me in such a humiliating position?* she fumed silently.

Wendy tipped Bob the usual amount and shut the door against the weather. "Oh, Winnie," she called from the living room in her best sugar-coated voice. "Could you come out here a minute, please?"

This time he was *really* going to get it!

Chapter
Three

"Wendy, I'm sorry. Okay?" Winston pleaded unhappily. "I'm sorry I got you a date with the man of your dreams, and I'm *inconsolable* that he sends you expensive flowers every week. I mean, how inconsiderate could I be? Any other girl I'd have fixed up with Pedro Paloma probably would have killed me by now."

"That's not funny, Winston," Wendy seethed.

"Come on, Wendy," Winston begged, abandoning his attempt at humor. "Don't you think you're overreacting just a *little?*"

"You weren't there!" Wendy practically shouted, and Winston could tell that she was fighting tears again—the way she always did when the flowers arrived. "I've never been so embarrassed in my life," she added in a shaking voice.

"Oh, Wendy." Winston put his arm around her and guided her from the front door toward a seat on the couch. "I really am sorry. I swear I never wanted to hurt you—I wanted to make you *happy*."

He removed the box of roses from his friend's trembling hands and set it on the coffee table as they sank side by side onto the sofa. Then Wendy buried her face in her hands and started crying for real.

"I don't know why you thought a *charity* date would make me happy," she managed to gasp. "Why would I want to go out with someone who had to be *forced* into being with me? Am I really that boring?"

"You're not boring at all," Winston assured her. "And so what if I kind of encouraged Pedro to ask you out? He decided he liked you all by himself. I never told him to send you flowers."

"You didn't *encourage* him, you *blackmailed* him," Wendy sobbed. "And he doesn't like me— he just feels guilty." She started crying even harder.

Winston assessed the deteriorating situation as best as he could. Sarcasm hadn't helped, and sympathy was making things worse. Desperate times called for desperate measures.

"Well, *I* think you're pretty terrific," Winston said, edging closer on the couch and drawing Wendy more tightly to his side. He stroked her long, sun-lightened brown hair gently, adoringly. "In fact, if I didn't already have a girlfriend, I think I'd have to . . . well, I'd have to . . ." He paused, waiting for just the right moment.

"Have to what?" Wendy sniffed at last, looking up.

"Tickle you!" Winston bellowed, knocking her over backward and attacking her around the ribs. She was still wearing her lifeguard suit under her unzipped jacket, and his fingers danced easily across the thin, slippery red fabric.

She started laughing almost immediately. "Winnie! Winnie, stop it!" she squealed. "Don't do that—I'm ticklish!"

"I was hoping you would be," he replied.

"Stop it! Stop it!" Wendy screamed with laughter. "You're going to make me wet my pants, I swear."

"There is no escape," Winston informed her in his best Dracula imitation as he pinned her squirming form to the sofa with his knees. "You must submit."

"Stop it, Winston. I mean it!"

Tears were pouring down her face now, but they were the tears of hysterical laughter. He decided to let her up.

"I will release you from my grip of terror under the condition that you acknowledge me, Winston the Worthy, Lord of the Universe," he told her, making his voice as deep and regal as possible. All those cartoons were good for something.

"You've got to be kidding," Wendy gasped, planting her hands against his chest and pushing

36

with surprising strength. Apparently she wasn't quite as helpless as he'd thought.

"All right, then," he agreed in his regular voice. "But you have to at *least* say 'uncle.'"

"Uncle!" Wendy capitulated immediately. "Now get *off* me."

"Be free, warrior princess!" Winston cried dramatically, rolling off the sofa and onto the floor. He acted as if he were doing her a big favor, but secretly he was relieved that she'd caved when she had. Wendy was in such good shape that he could barely hold her down.

"So are we friends again or what?" Winston asked her, rising to his feet and pretending to dust himself off—as if anyone could tell the difference the way he was dressed.

"Friends," Wendy agreed. "Until next time, anyway."

Winston lifted the roses from the coffee table and went through the swinging door into the kitchen to put them in water.

"You should give the poor guy a chance," he yelled back to Wendy, who was still recovering on the couch. "I really think he likes you."

"You can't possibly be dumb enough to want to start this conversation again," Wendy warned him, wandering into the kitchen and sitting on the counter. "I appreciate it about as much as you enjoy the why-don't-you-have-a-job-yet? inquisition. By the way, Winnie," she added, "why *don't* you have a job?"

Winston groaned out loud, momentarily stopping his search for a vase large enough to hold two dozen bloodred roses.

"Very funny."

"You *do* still *want* a job, don't you?" Wendy asked, sounding suspiciously like someone's mother. Apparently he wasn't done paying for the flower incident after all.

"You know I do," he answered, settling on a big wine carafe and filling it with water. "And I don't know why you're picking on me," he added. "I thought we were friends again."

"I'm not picking on you, Winston," Wendy replied. "I'm trying to help you. Hamburger Harry's just put a Help Wanted sign up. I heard that Harry's assistant manager had to move out of town unexpectedly."

"Assistant manager?" Winston echoed. That was the best-sounding job he'd heard about all summer. Sure, it was only a burger joint, but if he was the assistant *manager* . . .

"You ought to go down there *now*," Wendy told him. "Before someone else gets the job."

"You're right!" Winston agreed instantly, feeling better than he had for a month. First he would shower and shave, and then he'd put on his best khakis with a good shirt and his navy blazer. *Should I wear a tie, or would that be too formal?* he worried as he wandered distractedly in the direction of the living room. Halfway there he turned and walked back to where Wendy still sat on the counter, her bare feet dangling.

"Here," he said, forcing two dozen roses into her unwilling hands. "These are for you."

It felt good to be out of the wind, and Jessica sighed with pleasure as she curled her toes in the warm, soapy water of the pedicure tub. Even though she hadn't had an appointment, it had been easy to talk the receptionist at the beauty salon into fitting her in for an emergency manicure and pedicure—customers had been canceling appointments all morning on account of the horrible weather.

Jessica examined her freshly painted fingernails as her feet soaked in a mountain of bubbles. Soon the manicurist would return to finish the pedicure and polish her toenails to match. Jessica had decided on a bright red lacquer—perfect for the Fourth of July and sure to look great with the slinky, sapphire blue dress she'd just bought at that cute boutique on the corner. She glanced with satisfaction to where it sat in the open paper shopping bag at her side—a sheath of dark silk in a slip of white tissue.

All in all, this has been a good morning's work, Jessica congratulated herself. She'd convinced Nina to take her shift, Isabella was coming to visit, and—best of all—Elizabeth was about to get what she deserved. Jessica couldn't wait to see her twin's face when Tom showed up unexpectedly. Not to mention how available Ryan was going to be with poor Elizabeth all tied up . . .

Some sixth sense forced Jessica to turn her head just in time to see her housemate Ben strutting down the sidewalk, followed by his usual entourage of giggling girls. He *was* pretty cute, Jessica had to admit, but he was way too cocky. She just didn't see the attraction that had those other girls acting half mental with admiration. *Not wind nor sleet nor . . . how does that go again?* Jessica wondered, reminded for some reason of the Pony Express by the girls' empty-headed devotion. They even followed Ben around in a hurricane. Well, at least he wasn't bothering *her* for a change. That was something else she had to be happy about.

Of course just then he turned his head, and their eyes met and held through the plate-glass window. *Great,* Jessica groaned inwardly as she watched Ben dismiss his gaggle of admirers and stride confidently into the beauty shop. Jessica looked frantically for the manicurist to come to her rescue, but the woman was nowhere to be seen.

"Love the outfit," Ben opened in his deep voice, rolling up a manicurist's stool and sitting down to face her. "You should wear that tomorrow night."

Jessica's cheeks flamed as she realized what she had on. The black jeans she'd worn were too tight to roll up for a pedicure, so she'd shucked them off in favor of a wraparound, leopard-print smock provided by the salon. Everybody wore them—it was no big deal. At least it had never seemed like a big deal before.

"Glad you like it," she said rudely. "Maybe you could buy one for your admirers out there."

As usual he ignored her. The man was impossible to insult. Instead of leaving, he peeled off his lifeguard jacket and tossed it onto the floor beside his stool. Then he rolled in even closer.

"Aren't you supposed to be sick today?" he asked. "I could have sworn that Nina said you were dying or something."

Sick! she remembered in a rush, feeling momentarily queasy in spite of her perfect health. She *was* supposed to be sick. She'd forgotten all about it the moment Isabella had called.

"I felt horrible when I got up this morning," she lied moodily, "but I'm doing a little better now. Not that I owe *you* any explanations."

"None at all," he agreed. "You'd be much better off saving them for Nina."

"You're not going to tell her!" Jessica gasped in surprise. The guy was a pain, but ratting her out would be too low even for him.

"Maybe, maybe not," he said. "It depends."

"On what?" she asked suspiciously.

"On how nice you are to me."

Jessica could barely keep from groaning out loud. He had her, and he knew it.

41

"What do you want?" she asked, glaring. If she was lucky, maybe she could intimidate him into giving up.

But Ben only laughed at her. "So young, so beautiful, so cynical," he teased. "I just told you what I want. I want you to be nice to me."

"I don't know what you mean," Jessica informed him coldly. "I'm always nice."

"Sure you are," Ben agreed. "Nice to Ryan. Why don't you treat *me* like that for a change instead of mooning around after a guy who isn't worth the effort? You might find out you like me better than you think."

"I very much doubt it."

"That's exactly my point," Ben said. "You *doubt* it, but you don't *know.*"

"And you know so much, I suppose," Jessica returned sarcastically.

"I know that I'm crazy about you," Ben said sincerely, grabbing a towel from the manicurist's table beside them and spreading it across his navy blue sweatpants.

"What?" Jessica demanded, genuinely shocked.

But instead of answering, Ben reached into the tub full of bubbles. He grabbed one of her tanned ankles, lifting her left foot out and onto the towel in his lap.

"What are you doing?" she protested, struggling.

"Anything," he answered. "Anything for you."

His startling blue eyes bored intently into hers.

He means it! Jessica realized with a jolt. She stared back at him in disbelief, and for the first time since she'd met him, she saw something besides antagonism. Something deep, and sweet, and real. Something a girl could get used to. . . .

And then he got busy with the towel.

"I *would* dry them with my hair," he joked, massaging her foot in terry cloth, "but I don't think it's long enough." He ran a hand through his black crop cut for emphasis and flashed her a brilliant, crooked smile. Distractedly Jessica noticed how his untucked lifeguard T-shirt exposed just a sliver of tan, perfect abs. A lot of guys would have looked stupid with a girl's dripping foot in their lap, but not Ben—he looked absolutely adorable.

"What are you doing?" Jessica repeated in a whisper. It was unthinkable. Was she actually starting to *like* him?

"Well, I believe what comes next would be ze polishing," he said, affecting a truly horrible French accent. "Would mademoiselle prefer ze pink or ze red?"

"Ben!" she protested, trying to withdraw her foot from his lap.

"But of course! It is ze red, I see," he continued, glancing at her fingernails while holding her ankle tightly. He reached for the bottle of polish on the table. "If mademoiselle will be so good as

43

to hold still, I promise not to get any polish above ze knees." He opened the bottle one handed and held the dripping red brush over her foot like a dangerous weapon.

"Ben!" Jessica squealed, laughing. "Knock it off!"

"Never!" he declared, really hamming it up. "I am an arteest! I *must* paint zese little piggies!"

"Stop it!" she screeched, kicking soapsuds at him with her other foot. It was turning into a major disturbance as the two of them laughed and struggled. Jessica knew they were causing a scene, but she was having way too much fun to stop.

"Stop it, Ben," she screamed again. "I mean it!"

Nina had barely left the rental shop with her new surfboard under her arm when she'd realized she had a serious problem—there was no way she could hold on to the board long enough to walk home in the wind. She'd decided to go up Main Street as far as the pay phone and call Jessica to come get her, but to her surprise, no one had answered. Nina was heading back to the boardwalk to ask Paul if she could pick her board up later when she'd heard wild squeals of laughter coming out of the beauty salon she was passing. Squeals of Jessica Wakefield's laughter, to be exact.

That scheming little witch, Nina fumed, making her way through the door of the salon with her clumsy, oversize load. *She's not sick at all!* She immediately crossed to the manicure area and confronted her laughing, lying co-worker.

"Well, isn't this cozy?" Nina snapped. Jessica had one foot in a pedicure tub and one squirming foot in Ben's towel-covered lap. "What an *amazing* recovery."

"Nina!" Jessica blurted in reply. "What are you doing here?"

"I think that's the question *I* should be asking *you*," Nina replied. "If memory serves, I got up early to take your shift this morning because you were just burning up with fever."

Nina looked from Jessica's bare foot to Ben's smiling, satisfied face and back to Jessica's embarrassed, guilty one.

"The type of fever *you* have is pretty obvious," Nina told Jessica contemptuously, sizing up the situation with Ben. "And it's certainly no excuse for missing work."

"Oh, Nina! No!" Jessica exclaimed, looking truly horrified as she pulled her ankle from Ben's grasping hands. Nina noticed that she had to kick him in the gut to do it. "This isn't how it looks," Jessica explained. "Ben and I were only fooling around. I mean, not fooling *around*—forget about it! We were . . ."

"I don't care what you were doing," Nina cut her off. "I don't appreciate being used, Jessica. And don't think Ryan hasn't noticed how many

45

sick days you've taken, either. I used to think you could be a good lifeguard, but now it's obvious that you're blowing it."

Jessica stiffened visibly and her cheeks grew red. "You think you're so much better than everyone else," she accused. "If *you're* so conscientious, why aren't *you* at work?"

"In case you haven't noticed, there's a hurricane moving up from Baja. Ryan closed the beach and sent us home."

"Why aren't you at home, then?" Jessica asked rudely.

Nina bit her lip. Sometimes Jessica was too much.

"I would be," Nina said, trying to keep from shouting, "but I just bought this surfboard and I can't hang on to it in this wind. I need a ride."

"I'll take you," Ben volunteered immediately. "My car is right outside."

Jessica shot him what appeared to be a warning look.

"Thanks," Nina accepted gratefully. She had no beef with Ben, and if his taking her home annoyed Jessica for some reason, then that was even better.

As Nina turned to leave she saw Ben out of the corner of her eye, leaning down to whisper something to Jessica. She wasn't sure, but it looked like, "I told you so."

The glare Jessica gave Ben in return was so poisonous that Nina averted her eyes. Things had looked pretty lovey-dovey when she'd first walked in, but if those two were about to begin another of their wars, Nina wanted nothing to do with it.

Winston struggled down the boardwalk toward Hamburger Harry's with his head bowed into the wind. So much for the half hour he'd spent trying to gel his curls into submission—this weather was enough to blow the crease out of his pants. He was almost to Hamburger Harry's place when he ran into the South Beach Squad.

"Hey, *Winnie*," Kyle Fisher greeted him sarcastically. "What's little Winnie-the-Pooh doing out in a big bad storm like this?"

Rachel and some of the others tittered appreciatively.

Winston looked up as if he had just heard something amazing. "Wow," he said earnestly. "Does someone have a pencil? That's so original I want to write it down."

Peter Horton and Mickey Esposito laughed. They weren't as bad as the rest of the guys on the squad—especially Kyle. Winston hated him *and* his stupid fishing hat.

"Going swimming this weekend, Winnie?" nasty Danielle Dodge asked, moving to block his way. "Better get some water wings. We're going to be too busy with the tourists to waste our time rescuing ninety-pound weaklings like you."

Winston considered pushing her out of his way,

but decided she could probably take him. He'd never seen a bigger, more muscle-bound girl in his life.

"For your information," he sniffed, "I wouldn't swim at *your* pathetic beach if you paid me. And anyway, I'm just as good a swimmer as any of you."

The rest of the group laughed hysterically, but Rachel stepped forward, suddenly serious.

"You want to bet?" she asked him. "How much?"

"Who's going to race me?" Winston bluffed, wishing he'd kept his big mouth shut.

"We'll *all* race out to the buoy and back," Rachel proposed. "If you beat any one of us, you win."

"Hey!" Kristi Bjorn protested. "I don't think anyone should be swimming in this weather. It's not safe."

"I'll go," Tina Fong offered immediately.

"What do you say, Winston?" Rachel pressed.

Rachel always wanted to make bets—especially when it was a sure thing, Winston noted unhappily. The greed in her eyes this time was so transparent that Winston had a feeling she'd match any sum he named. For a second he actually considered taking her bet—after all, he only had to beat one of them, and anything could happen. Then he looked out at the water. The ocean had worked itself into a frothy gray so dark it was almost black.

And the chop was so high he couldn't even *see* the buoy. Who was he fooling? They'd kick his butt.

"Some other time," he brushed her off, straightening his blazer lapels importantly. "Right now I have to see a gentleman about a job."

He could still hear them jeering as he turned off the boardwalk onto the pier and finally reached the door to Hamburger Harry's. *I hope the Sweet Valley Shore Squad kills them in the merit-pay competition,* he thought vindictively as he walked into the restaurant.

Winston took a second just inside the door to compose himself, straightening his tie and smoothing his hair before he approached the guy behind the counter.

"I'd like to speak to Mr. . . . uh . . . Harry," Winston announced. He could feel his cheeks burning with embarrassment at his ill-thought-out opening. *Great start so far,* he chided himself.

The pudgy, dark-haired man behind the counter looked him over critically. Winston guessed he was about thirty, based primarily on the receding hairline. "And you would be . . . ?" the counter guy asked, wiping his hands on a greasy apron.

"Winston Egbert. Please tell Harry that I'm here about the assistant manager's position."

The guy behind the counter laughed. "I don't know what you've been smoking, kid, but there's no assistant manager's position." He gestured with the knife he'd been using to slice tomatoes when Winston walked in. "Does it look like we need one?"

The tiny restaurant on the pier was completely empty. It was built to take maximum advantage of the view, with an outdoor deck on three sides, but all Winston could see through the enormous windows was the rapidly worsening storm.

"Well, not today," Winston acknowledged, trying not to get whiny. "But I'm sure you do better in good weather. If I could only speak to Harry—"

"*I'm* Harry," the guy cut him off, extending his hand. "What do you think? I have a cast of thousands?"

Winston took Harry's hand and held on to it like a lifeline.

"I need a job," he said desperately. "I'm smart, and I learn really fast. Not only that, I'm a whiz with figures if you have any bookkeeping or accounting you need done."

Harry seemed unimpressed.

"You *do* have a Help Wanted sign in the window," Winston added, dropping Harry's hand and pointing. His heart pounded painfully and a nervous sweat trickled down his neck as he waited for Harry's response.

"Yeah," Harry said slowly, a smile spreading over his slightly crooked features. "That's right, I do. I'm afraid it isn't assistant manager, but I'll bet a bright guy like you understands that you can't always start at the top. You've got to get your foot in the door first. Prove yourself, if you know what I mean."

Winston pounced on the opportunity. "You are *so* right, sir," he agreed. "Of course I understand all about that."

"Call me Harry," Harry told him, stepping out from behind the counter. "You know, Winston, I think I have a job for you after all."

"Really?" Winston's hopes soared.

"Yep, I do. A smart guy, a quick learner like yourself—you'd be perfect for it."

"Thank you, sir! Uh, I mean Harry," Winston fumbled, grabbing his new boss's hand again and pumping it enthusiastically. "When can I start?"

Harry smiled again. "As a matter of fact, you can start right now."

Chapter Four

Ryan stopped the Jeep at the beach house curb and Elizabeth hopped out thankfully, her blond pony-tail whipping in the increasingly violent storm. Since the moment their hands had clenched so briefly on the gearshift, Ryan had maintained a near total silence. Elizabeth mumbled her good-bye and then ran into the house.

What's wrong with him? she asked herself as she struggled to keep a grip on the bucking front door. *What's wrong with me?* She managed to close the door behind her, then immediately crossed to the living-room window to see if the Jeep was still there. It wasn't, and Elizabeth sighed heavily. She was more confused than ever.

"Stinky, huh?" Nina asked, startling her. Elizabeth spun around to see her best friend sitting by herself on the sofa. Even though she knew Nina was referring to the weather, right then she could as easily have been talking about Elizabeth's love life.

"How about making some popcorn with me and hanging out in the kitchen?" Nina suggested before Elizabeth could answer.

"Thanks," Elizabeth agreed, smiling. "That sounds great."

Nina smiled back, and Elizabeth was suddenly reminded how nice it was to look into an open, friendly face—especially after spending the last agonizing hour looking at Ryan's closed, moody one. She stripped off her jacket as she followed Nina into the kitchen. The two girls were dressed identically in their lifeguard-issue gear, but Elizabeth had always thought that the bright orange jackets flattered Nina's dark brown, African American complexion more than hers.

"I have a feeling that by the time I get a brush through this mess, I'm going to wish I had beads like yours," Elizabeth griped, putting a hand to her silky blond snarls. She sank into a chair at the kitchen table while Nina searched the back of the cupboard for a package of microwave popcorn she'd hidden from the guys.

"It's been done," Nina reminded her. "Remember Bo Derek in '10'?"

"Who could forget?" Elizabeth groaned. "If I thought braiding my hair would make Ryan act as crazy for me as Dudley Moore was over her, I'd do it in a second."

It was out of her mouth before she'd even realized she was going to say it. Elizabeth stared horrified at Nina, dreading her friend's reaction.

"Actually, it takes most of the day to do a good braid job," Nina said casually. "*And* a considerable amount of money." She tossed the popcorn into the microwave and set the timer for three minutes.

"What?" Elizabeth asked.

"Getting your hair braided like mine," Nina explained. "And it's harder with soft, straight hair like yours. I tried to do a friend's once in high school and it turned out awful."

"Nina, did you hear what I just said?" Elizabeth demanded.

"I heard you," Nina said, taking a chair beside her. "So what do you want me to say? That I think you're a terrible person?"

With a guilty start Elizabeth realized that was exactly what she wanted her friend to say. If Nina couldn't talk her out of wanting Ryan, who could?

"Don't you think I am?" Elizabeth asked, surprised.

"Maybe," Nina said. "And maybe you're only human. You're certainly no worse than anybody else."

The timer chimed on the microwave, startling them both. Nina rose to pour the steaming popcorn into a bowl, and the familiar aroma filled the kitchen as she put it on the table between them.

They ate for a few moments in silence while

Elizabeth studied her friend. She'd been so caught up in her own problems that she'd never even noticed something was bothering Nina. But now it was obvious. Elizabeth couldn't believe she hadn't noticed before.

"Is something wrong?" Elizabeth asked, concerned. "Did something happen?"

"No. Yes. I don't know," Nina said. "It's just that lately I don't know if I'm coming or going."

"I know how *that* feels," Elizabeth said, her thoughts returning to Ryan. But why would Nina be confused? Then suddenly, she knew.

"It's Paul, isn't it?" Elizabeth asked.

Nina nodded miserably. "I'm just so torn," she explained. "I mean, I love Bryan."

"I know how you feel."

"Really?" Nina asked hopefully.

"Absolutely," Elizabeth assured her. "Are you telling yourself at least ten times a day that you already have the world's greatest boyfriend?"

Nina nodded.

"That you're crazy to even look at someone else?" Elizabeth continued.

Nina confirmed it with another nod.

"That only an *idiot* would throw away a special, caring relationship with a guy she loves for the sake of a summer fling?"

"That pretty much sums it up," Nina agreed.

"*Boy,* do I know how you feel," Elizabeth commiserated. How ironic that she and Nina, two of the most loyal, responsible people she knew, would find themselves in the same predicament.

"So, are you and Ryan going to get together or what?" Nina asked finally.

"I don't know."

"Hey! I *thought* I smelled popcorn," Ben bellowed, pushing through the kitchen door. "Thanks for inviting me, you guys," he added sarcastically.

"We didn't think you'd want any," Elizabeth improvised. "It's low fat."

"In this life you take what you can get and get what you can take." Ben pulled up a chair. "At least that's my new philosophy. I made it up this morning. What do you think?"

"Very deep," Elizabeth said, smiling.

Ben plunged a hand into the popcorn bowl and began transferring the contents to his mouth. "So what are you girls talking about?" he asked. "Me, I hope."

That was vain even for Ben.

"Why, yes," Nina teased in return. "Just before you walked in here, Elizabeth and I were both saying what a total studmuffin you are."

"Thank you, ladies." He grinned. "You may continue."

"It's practically tragic that you have your heart so set on the enchanting Jessica Wakefield," Nina went on. She heaved an enormous fake sigh and batted her lashes at him.

"What's *tragic* is that she can't get her mind

off the enchanting Ryan Taylor," Ben grumbled, losing interest in the game. "He's never going to go out with her—he's totally self-absorbed."

"Yes. Well," Elizabeth said uncomfortably. "I just remembered I promised to call my parents this weekend. I think I'll do it now."

But once she'd escaped to her room, Elizabeth felt no desire to talk to her mom and dad. The person she *wanted* to talk to was Ryan. She thought about their awkward ride together in the Jeep—her unsuccessful attempts to make conversation and his determined silences. *I should have made him tell me how he feels,* she thought. *I should have found out what he wants.* It all seemed so clear now in the safety of her room, but when she'd faced him earlier, she'd been scared to death.

Scared of what? she asked herself. *What am I so afraid of?*

But she already knew. She was afraid Ryan didn't feel about her the way she did about him. She had already risked so much to be with him— the thought of how she was betraying Tom made her ill. Ryan *had* to feel the same way she felt! So why was he so withdrawn, so secretive? It threw her off balance.

She sat down on her bed and tried to think. She couldn't let things continue the way they were—the wondering, the not knowing, the wanting him. . . . It was driving her crazy. Maybe Elizabeth and Ryan were meant for each other and maybe they weren't, but Elizabeth had to know.

She sprang off her bed with sudden determination.

"That's it," she announced aloud, heading for her closet. She was going to change into some regular clothes, and then she was going to drop in on Ryan. She had to get things straightened out between them. *Today.*

Jessica walked out of the beauty salon and into a whirlwind. The weather had become truly frightening while they'd finished her pedicure, but she was in such a foul mood that she barely noticed.

Ben's a total loser! she thought as she made her way down the windy sidewalk, trying to keep the string handles of the twisting paper shopping bag from ruining her still wet nail polish. For about five minutes in the beauty salon, she'd almost liked him. He'd actually been charming. But he'd shown his true colors again the second Nina had walked in.

"Oh, *I'll* take you home, Nina," Jessica mocked him out loud as she turned north onto the boardwalk. "I'd *love* to."

What a pig. If he was any kind of a man at all, he would have said he was already driving Jessica. Now she had to walk home. She could barely hold on to her shopping bag in the gusty wind, and it was starting to rain, too. By the time she got home, her new silk dress would probably be ruined.

I'll get him for this, she promised herself.

Just then she spotted someone walking toward her on the boardwalk. Rachel. *The two of them are like a curse!* Jessica thought. There was no way she was going to deal with Rachel right then if she could avoid it. Quickly she ducked inside the very next shop she came to.

The bells hanging on the door rang crazily in the wild winds as Jessica first opened and then slammed it shut behind her. The bells struck her as unusual, but it wasn't until she turned around that Jessica saw they were the most normal thing in the room.

She was in Madame Wolenska's—the fortune-teller's shop. The walls were painted black, and the drawn curtains were a heavy, blood-colored velvet. The only pieces of furniture in the room were a few antique-looking tapestry chairs and a large black velvet-draped table, behind which sat a tiny turbaned and bespectacled Madame Wolenska.

Great, Jessica thought, wishing she had landed in any other store on the boardwalk. She'd never been to the fortune-teller's place before, but she'd heard plenty about it. Everyone said the old lady was a total kook.

"Hello, Jessica," Madame Wolenska said from her place behind the table. "I had a feeling I'd meet you today."

She had no sooner spoken than a huge crack of lightning cleaved the sky. The thunder that followed rattled the windows as it rumbled through the street.

"M-meet me?" Jessica stammered, spooked by the strangeness of her surroundings and the timing of the lightning. "You don't even *know* me. How do you know my name?"

"I know all things," Madame Wolenska said simply. "But it's also embroidered on your jacket."

Of course! Jessica had put on her lifeguard jacket when she'd left the salon. She almost laughed with relief.

"Come, sit down," Madame Wolenska urged, motioning her to come forward. "We have a lot to talk about."

"Oh, I don't want my fortune told," Jessica demurred. "Actually, I was just trying to get away from the weather."

Madame Wolenska smiled. "Well, you were trying to get away from *something*. That part's true."

Suddenly Jessica was creeped out again. Could this strange old woman really know she'd been avoiding Rachel?

"Trying to get away from what?" Jessica challenged, hoping her voice didn't betray her. She was finding the entire encounter to be way too weird.

"From your destiny, I would imagine," Madame Wolenska said. "That's what most people are running from. Now come and sit down. Please, please." She gestured more insistently at the empty chair across from her.

"*I* believe we make our *own* destinies," Jessica announced as she sat reluctantly at the table with Madame Wolenska. *Up close the scariest thing about her is that turquoise eye shadow,* Jessica thought, stifling a giggle.

"I've been seeing you for several days," Madame Wolenska said. "You come to me when I sleep. You have a sister, no? One who looks just like you?"

"Yes," Jessica admitted uneasily.

"But you are the strong one," Madame Wolenska continued. "This is why I see *you.* I see you trying to change the lives of the people around you in order to change your own. That is always very dangerous, Jessica."

"Oh, *please,*" Jessica protested, getting more uncomfortable by the second.

"May I see your hand?" inquired Madame Wolenska.

"What for?" Jessica asked suspiciously, putting them under the table.

"Yes. I saw that too." The old lady sighed. "You are strong, but you are full of fear. It is your fear that drives you."

"That's ridiculous." Jessica extended her hand immediately. "I have nothing to be afraid of. And watch the nail polish," she added. "It's still a little wet."

Madame Wolenska ignored her as she began reading her palm. "I see an important man in your life. A strong man—a match for you in every way. I know," she interrupted herself, looking up and smiling, "we psychics are always seeing a man. But this one isn't in your future—he's in your present. You see him or speak to him or think about him every day."

Ryan, Jessica thought immediately. He was a strong man and they *would* be a perfect match!

"I see also that there have been problems between you and this man. Things are not going the way they should."

Definitely Ryan, Jessica interjected silently. *If things were going the way they should, he'd be my boyfriend by now.*

"Yes!" Madame Wolenska said suddenly, sucking in her breath. "Here it is."

"There *what* is?" Jessica asked, her interest growing.

"Here is the thing I was looking for—the thing that came to me in my dreams," Madame Wolenska said. "It is very special. Very rare."

"What?" Jessica urged. She was hanging on the old woman's every word now.

"You and this man were married in a past life, and now you've found each other again."

"Married!" Jessica exclaimed.

"Yes. But it ended very badly."

"Are you sure you're not seeing my marriage in *this* life?" Jessica quipped, thinking of her ex-husband, Michael McAllery.

But Madame Wolenska became unexpectedly angry. "This is not to joke about," she said with unexpected passion. "And I know what I see. The marriage you refer to was nothing—an infatuation—compared to this one. And now you have this precious, precious chance to right old wrongs and you are throwing it away."

"No, I'm not," Jessica assured her. "I'm doing everything I can for this guy, but he's—"

Madame Wolenska cut her off. "You do *nothing* for this man," she scolded. "In fact, by the end of the weekend you will hurt him very badly. You have no concept of destiny—his *or* yours. You are full of your own petty plans, are you not?"

But Jessica had heard enough. Jerking her hand out of Madame Wolenska's, she backed away from the table and ran out into the storm just as another bolt of lightning cracked.

The rain was pouring down in huge, wind-driven drops, but Jessica barely noticed it as she ran blindly down the boardwalk, her shopping bag clasped to her chest. That fortune-teller was wrong. She had to be! Jessica would never do anything to hurt Ryan—in this life or any other.

Suddenly she remembered her plan to have Tom show up unexpectedly the next morning, and her stomach lurched. *But that isn't meant to hurt Ryan,* she assured herself. *It's for his own good. He and Liz are a joke together—he needs to see her with Tom to understand how unavailable she is.*

For a second Jessica felt reassured, but only for a second. Madame Wolenska's words still rang strangely in her ears: *You have a precious chance to right old wrongs and you are throwing it away.*

That can't be right! Jessica thought, becoming increasingly frantic. The storm, Madame Wolenska, her fears for Ryan all fueled her steps as she flew down the rain-slick boardwalk at top running speed.

Suddenly Jessica knew what she had to do. She had to see Ryan, and right away. He was sure to be at the Main Tower, and it was about time the two of them got things out in the open. He was never meant to be Elizabeth's; he was *hers.* Jessica knew it, Madame Wolenska knew it, and soon Ryan would know it too.

Jessica reached the end of the boardwalk and leapt off at a dead run, landing in the soft wet sand below. She barely noticed the cramp in her side as she ran full tilt in the direction of Ryan's tower.

"I just don't understand why you won't talk about it," Elizabeth persisted unhappily. "Why do you keep shutting me out?"

She looked at Ryan. He was motionless at the window, his binoculars trained on what he could see of the water through the raging storm outside. Even though the beach was officially closed, Ryan refused to go down to his room, remaining instead on voluntary watch in the glassed-in portion of the tower.

He wouldn't even look at her. Elizabeth felt as if she were watching their only chance at happiness fall apart before her eyes.

"Will you please put down those binoculars and *talk* to me?" she pleaded, fighting tears.

"I told you this morning. I think it's better if we don't get involved."

"But you didn't say *why*," Elizabeth protested.

Suddenly Ryan's broad, muscular back stiffened. "Oh, sh . . ." he gasped, dropping the binoculars onto the counter and stripping off his jacket.

"What? What is it?" Elizabeth asked, but he was already out the door. She watched as Ryan struggled to kick off his sweatpants as he grabbed the orange rescue buoy from the railing. Freeing his legs, he jumped from the tower to the sand below and began streaking toward the water.

"Oh no," Elizabeth exclaimed, grabbing the binoculars. "Someone must be out there."

At first all she could see through the rain were Ryan's red trunks and his strong, powerful arms as they sliced through the whitecaps. She focused the binoculars a little ways in front of him. Nothing. She looked out farther. Still nothing. Frantically she returned her view to Ryan. He was a hundred yards offshore now, passing the buoys in the worst conditions Elizabeth had ever seen. She had to help him, but she didn't even know what he was doing. She aimed the binoculars as far out to sea as she could make out, squinting to see something, anything. And that was when she found the tiny black speck in the water that was the top of someone's head.

"I don't believe it," she gasped, the binoculars slipping from her hands. The swimmer was so far out that Elizabeth couldn't even tell if it was a guy or a girl, a kid or an adult. Whoever it was must have been caught in a rip current and swept out to sea. And that meant that getting back in by swimming straight toward the sand was going to be impossible—especially if it had to be done while dragging someone else. The only way to get to shore would be to swim sideways far enough to clear the current and then turn in toward the beach. It would be an exhausting, dangerous rescue under the best of conditions—Ryan was on a suicide mission.

Barely hesitating, Elizabeth stripped to her pale pink bra and underwear. Then she got on the radio and put out an emergency call:

"This is Elizabeth Wakefield, Sweet Valley Shore Lifeguard Squad. We're attempting an emergency rescue in dangerous conditions. There are two lifeguards and one victim in the water approximately five hundred yards off the Main Tower. Over."

She knew she should wait for a response, but

there was no time. In a flash she was down the tower stairs and grabbing the rescue board from its rack. The big paddle board would keep them on top of the current, making it easier to get back in. *If nothing else, at least it will float us all until the Harbor Patrol can send out a boat,* Elizabeth thought grimly as she raced across the sand.

The chill of the ocean barely registered as Elizabeth launched herself into the surf, but the size of the waves got her attention instantly. The storm surf was huge, ugly, and confused. It seemed as if it was coming from every direction at once, and Elizabeth ducked her head repeatedly as the breaking waves crashed over the board, smashing her under and filling her nose and mouth with black, suffocating water.

I've got to keep paddling, she told herself, desperately fighting her fear. *Ryan needs me.*

If she could get past the surf line, Elizabeth knew the going would be easier. Finally she crested the last major swell and, as she rose, she saw that Ryan was almost to the swimmer. She could also see that he was already exhausted from swimming unaided through the heavy seas.

Hurry, hurry, hurry, her brain chanted in time to her arms. She sped through the water faster than she would have dreamed possible. The adrenaline pumped through her veins, pushing her to new limits. At last the swimmer came into view again—it was a girl. Ryan had her in a chin hold and was struggling to swim sideways out of the rip current so that he could work his way back in. The rescue buoy trailed on its line behind him, useless for anything except emergency flotation.

"Ryan!" Elizabeth shouted against the wind.

He looked up as she rushed toward him on the rescue board.

"What are you doing out here?" he demanded roughly, but she could see the relief in his eyes.

"Saving your butt," she replied. "Get on."

Instead Ryan maneuvered his teenage victim toward the front of the big board. Elizabeth saw that she was terrified but fully conscious. Ryan pushed from behind as Elizabeth reached out and grabbed the girl by one arm.

"Ow!" the girl screamed as Elizabeth began to pull. "My shoulder!"

"Then give me your other hand," Elizabeth told her as she and Ryan half pushed, half pulled the frightened victim out of the water and onto her stomach on the front of the board.

"I'm okay," the girl gasped before Elizabeth could even ask her. She took a few deep breaths, trying to calm herself. "It's just my shoulder," she explained. "And I lost my equipment."

"What equipment?" Elizabeth asked, lying over the girl's back and beginning to paddle. She wanted to keep her talking to see if she was in shock. Ryan, meanwhile, had gone around to grip the tail of the board and was in the water kicking while Elizabeth used her arms.

"My board, mast, sail. Everything, I guess," the girl said through chattering teeth. She was wearing a slick black spring suit, but she was obviously still freezing.

Elizabeth couldn't hide her amazement. "You were out here *windsurfing!*" she exclaimed. "By yourself?"

"Yeah. It looked pretty wild," said the girl. "You know, once-in-a-lifetime conditions and all that. It was killer, too, until I wiped out. My board got blown away from me faster than I could swim for it."

The rescue board crested a swell, and Elizabeth could see they were still a long way from shore.

"What's your name?" Elizabeth asked.

"Kim. Kim Aquino."

"How long have you been sailing, Kim?" Ryan asked from behind them.

"About six months," she answered.

"Six months!" Ryan exploded. "Are you crazy?"

"Yeah," Kim said, immediately sheepish. "I must be. I'm really sorry you guys had to come rescue me."

"We're not out of the water yet," Ryan reminded her.

Finally they reached the surf line and then, mercifully, the beach. The last wave knocked Elizabeth and Kim sideways off the board, but they held on by the edge and were soon on the sand, Ryan right behind them. Kim immediately sat down and began to shiver uncontrollably, all the while gripping her injured right shoulder.

"I'm going for the Jeep," Ryan told Elizabeth, who was crouching at Kim's side. "I'm taking her to the hospital."

Elizabeth stood up. "I'm going with you," she told him, expecting an argument and ready to win it.

But Ryan was staring at her as if he'd never seen her before in his life.

"What?" she asked, looking down. Her cheeks flamed brilliantly as she realized she was standing there in her bra and underwear. Wet underwear. And even though her pink lingerie had been reasonably modest dry, wet and clinging was an entirely different, much more transparent story.

When she looked back up, Ryan was already running through the rain toward the tower. Elizabeth bent again to check on their victim.

"He's gone for the Jeep so we can take you to the hospital," she told Kim. "I just want to make sure he picks up some blankets. Will you be okay without me a minute?"

The girl nodded, her long black braid still streaming salt water.

"I'll hurry," Elizabeth promised, turning and racing across the sand.

Just as Elizabeth reached the tower, Ryan met

her at the bottom of the steps, the Jeep keys in his hands. He had thrown his orange lifeguard jacket on over his wet red trunks and his arms were already full of blankets.

"Come here," he ordered, holding a blanket spread open in his arms.

It was no time to be shy, Elizabeth knew. She stepped quickly forward and he wrapped her in the blanket, squeezing her tight for warmth. She imagined she could feel the heat of his bare chest radiating through the blanket as she snuggled deeply into his embrace, wishing he'd never let her go.

"You're shivering," he said. "Are you okay?"

"I will be," she answered, clinging to him tightly, her legs suddenly numb beneath her. The full magnitude of what they'd just accomplished broke over her like one of the cresting storm surges.

"Are we great lifeguards or what?" she whispered, smiling happily into his eyes.

Running through the soft sand in the pouring rain had really slowed Jessica down, but she was finally within sight of the Main Tower. The cramp in her side had become a searing ache and her lungs felt ready to burst, but in another minute it would all be worth it. Jessica could practically feel Ryan's strong arms around her, his passionate lips against hers. She cleared the final rise before the tower and stopped short, horrified at the sight before her.

Elizabeth and Ryan were standing together at the base of the stairs and . . . no, it was too unbelievable. Was Elizabeth wearing a bra and *underpants?* Jessica saw just enough to be sure of it before Ryan enveloped her sister first in a blanket and then in his arms. Elizabeth melted up against him as they gazed into each other's eyes, oblivious to everything else around them.

How could I have been so stupid? Jessica asked herself furiously, turning her back on the scene at the tower and stumbling blindly through the sand the way she had come. The wind was wicked, and the air was filled with strange wails, creaks, and thumps, but Jessica paid no attention as she hurried toward home. Elizabeth *was* cheating on Tom! Jessica had known it all along.

Well, I think it's time Tom found out too, Jessica decided, a new, more direct plan taking shape in her mind. *The second I get home, I'm going to call Tom and tell . . .*

The violent blow to the side of Jessica's head was so sudden that she barely felt the pain before the blackness engulfed her and she dropped unconscious to the sand.

Chapter Five

"I'm really worried, Ben," Nina confided, staring anxiously out the front window. The afternoon was becoming late, and the sky was getting darker. She wouldn't have thought it possible, but it was raining even harder than before, and lightning streaked the sky at regular intervals now. "I wish Elizabeth hadn't gone back out in this," Nina added.

"Uh-huh," Ben agreed distractedly.

Nina turned to look at him. Ben stood beside her at the window. He seemed every bit as worried as she was, but he also looked like he hadn't heard a word she'd said.

"Do you think she's okay?" Nina asked, wanting reassurance.

"I hope so," he said fervently. "I wish like anything we'd waited for her and driven her home from town."

"What?" Nina asked, confused. "She didn't go

to town—she went to the tower to see Ryan, re-member?"

"No," Ben corrected her, "*Elizabeth* went to see Ryan."

"That's what I just said!" Nina exclaimed. "She went to the tower. I'm really worried."

"Yeah," Ben agreed, without much interest. It was as if he were having some entirely different conversation.

Then all of a sudden he brought his hand down on the windowsill so hard it made Nina jump.

"Of *course* she went to the tower!" he exclaimed, already grabbing his coat off the sofa. "Nina, you're a genius."

"What are you talking about?" Nina protested, totally confused, but Ben was opening the front door out into the screeching wind and rain. "Ben, where are you going?"

"I'm just going to go check on *Elizabeth*," he replied, "to make sure she's okay. Back soon."

Nina watched from the window as Ben fought down the walkway to his car and drove off through the pouring rain.

I hope he finds her and brings her home, Nina worried, chewing at the edge of a fingernail without realizing what she was doing. It was scary being the only one in the house. The old wooden Victorian was creaking like it was going to come apart any second, and there was water leaking through the kitchen windows and the ceilings of both Wendy and Jessica's rooms. It had been Ben's idea to check for roof leaks—Nina had just helped him scrounge up enough buckets and cooking pots to catch the drops.

That's what I'll do, Nina decided, taking her finger from her mouth. *I'll go empty the buckets. It will be better than standing here and waiting.*

She turned her back to the window and walked toward the stairs, but she was still only on the second flight when she heard something pounding against the house. She paused—could that be someone at the door? Almost immediately someone leaned on the doorbell, holding it down until it buzzed.

"All right!" she said out loud, starting back down the stairs. She had barely begun when the doorbell sounded again, longer this time.

Nina started to run, her heart pounding. Something must be really wrong. Bounding off the bottom step and flying across the living room, she unlocked the front door and threw it open. There on the porch stood Paul, the large, limp form of Paloma Perro draped across his arms.

They were both soaked. Paul's drenched red shirt clung to his chest and shoulders, and water streamed from his short black hair, but it was poor Paloma who looked truly pitiful—his shaggy, multicolored fur lay plastered to his lifeless body.

"Oh no!" Nina gasped, horrified. She grabbed Paul by his elbow and dragged him inside. "What

75

happened? He's not . . . ?" She couldn't even bring herself to say it.

"Not yet," Paul said, his dark eyes worried, "but I'm not sure he's going to make it, either. We've got to get him to a vet right away."

"But what happened?" Nina repeated in a wail. She imagined how Wendy would react if Nina had to tell her that her dog had died unexpectedly, and felt instantly sick to her stomach.

"I don't know," Paul said briefly, and for the first time Nina noticed the strain in his voice. "I just found him lying under your front porch with a bunch of these." He flexed one big hand up from underneath the mutt, and Nina saw that it held an uncooked hot dog. "Maybe they were bad or something," Paul suggested.

"But where did he *get* those?" Nina demanded, near tears.

"I don't know," Paul answered again, "but if we don't get him to the vet soon, I've got a feeling it'll all be academic. He's in bad shape, Nina."

"You're right," she agreed immediately, pulling herself together. "Just let me leave a note for Wendy."

She ran into the kitchen and dashed off a note on the pad by the telephone, then hurried back to where Paul stood patiently waiting, the heavy, unconscious dog still cradled gently in his arms. Nina felt her heart turn over. Paul was such a great guy—so caring, so kind—how could loving him be wrong?

76

"Come on," she said, hoping he wouldn't notice the sudden constriction in her throat. She opened the front door and together they ran through the rain toward Paul's blue Toyota pickup.

This isn't exactly what I had in mind, Winston finally admitted to himself. The wind and rain knocked him around like a toy in his giant hamburger costume, and he could barely keep his footing on the slick wooden surface of the boardwalk. To top it off, the hamburger leaked—a lot. *It's not bad enough having Eat at Hamburger Harry's painted across my buns?* Winston asked himself. *I have to have soggy lettuce too?*

Harry had really sucked him in. Winston knew that now. All that talk about how bright Winston was and getting in on the ground floor was the only thing that had kept Winston from walking out the restaurant door the second he'd heard what Harry had in mind. He couldn't wear a stupid hamburger costume for the tourists—he'd be as bad as Hot Dog Howie!

But Harry had been persuasive. "This is just a stepping-stone to bigger and better things," he'd wheedled. "If you do the hamburger guy bit for the weekend, I'll give you a regular job on Tuesday," he'd promised.

It's just temporary, Winston reminded himself. Despite the fact that the driving rain had just found a way to come in through the back of his costume and trickle down his underwear, he smiled at the thought of actually having some money soon.

The lightning strike that hit the beach a few seconds later brought him back to his senses with a bang. Winston had never seen lightning actually touch the ground before. What he was doing wasn't just dumb, it was *stupid*. It was also completely pointless—there was no one around to see him for miles. Winston turned in his tracks and beat a fast retreat back to Hamburger Harry's.

"I quit!" Winston announced loudly the second he entered the restaurant.

Harry had apparently given up on serving any customers that afternoon. He was sitting at a corner table, drinking coffee—the steaming pot rested on a trivet in front of him, filling the room with its warm, comforting smell.

"I don't blame you," Harry replied. "I was nuts to send you out in this weather. It was a total waste of your time and talent."

"Not to mention dangerous and stupid," Winston sniffed.

"You're right," Harry agreed. "Completely. Come sit down and have a cup of coffee."

Harry gestured to the seat on the other side of the little square table, and Winston noticed for the first time that there was an extra mug waiting. He could practically taste the hot, reviving coffee as he started for the chair. . . .

Wait a minute! he reminded himself. He was supposed to be quitting.

"I said I quit," Winston repeated.

"Yeah," Harry said mildly. "I heard you the first time. Does that mean you're giving up coffee, too?"

"Well, no," Winston admitted, surprised that Harry wasn't going to try to talk him out of it. "I guess not."

"So, what then?" Harry demanded. "You hate me now? We can't even have coffee together?"

"Of course I don't hate you," Winston assured him. How could he have been so rude? "Just let me put on something dry."

Winston ran for the tiny back room of the restaurant and changed quickly back into his khakis and jacket, leaving the sodden hamburger suit hanging on a peg to dry for the next poor sucker. Grabbing a clean dish towel off a metal rack, he toweled his hair as well as he could and then finger combed it straight back, shivering as cold droplets ran under his dry shirt collar. When he finally rejoined Harry in the dining room, he was really looking forward to that cup of hot coffee.

"You look better," Harry observed as he poured coffee into Winston's cup and pushed the sugar and cream in his direction.

"I *feel* better," Winston said, stirring in plenty of both. "No offense, but that was the stupidest job I've ever had in my life."

Winston half expected Harry to get mad, but he just laughed pleasantly. "I don't doubt it. A smart guy like you was made for better things."

"I'm glad you agree," Winston told him, taking a huge gulp of the sweetened, creamy coffee. *A couple of cups of this and I might feel almost human again,* he thought.

"I can't even tell you how many guys I've hired that couldn't cut it in the suit," Harry said kindly. "You shouldn't be ashamed about quitting—it's good to know your limitations."

"What?" Winston squeaked, outraged. "I didn't say I couldn't cut it; I—"

"No," Harry interrupted, holding up a hand to stop him. "There's no need for explanations. I understand."

"You do not!" Winston protested.

"It *is* a shame, though," Harry continued, undeterred, "because I was watching you from the window here while there were still a few tourists on the boardwalk. You're the best I've ever seen. I was *proud* to have you wear my suit."

"Uh, thank you," Winston said, utterly confused.

"You blow Hot Dog Howie away," Harry said. "And I'm not just saying that. Really. You're a natural talent."

"Thanks," Winston repeated, sucking down some more coffee.

The situation was bizarre, and yet Winston couldn't help feeling a certain glow of accomplishment. He *did* blow Hot Dog Howie away—it was nice that someone had noticed.

"I'll bet tomorrow, if it's sunny, you'll reel in the tourists like fish," Harry said, pouring more coffee into Winston's empty cup.

"Yeah," Winston agreed dreamily, imagining the look on Hot Dog Howie's face when he found out he had some *real* competition for a change. Then he remembered.

"Hey!" he protested. "I already quit, remember?"

"I remember," Harry said. "Want to be rehired? It's only for the weekend, and then I'll let you cook or cashier or something, like we said."

"No way," Winston said firmly. "I never would have let you talk me into doing that bit in the first place if I wasn't so broke."

"Money was the *only* reason you took the hamburger guy job?" Harry asked, watching Winston closely.

Winston looked straight into his ex-boss's watery eyes and nodded emphatically.

"Then I'll double it," Harry offered smoothly. "But only for the weekend."

Winston was shocked—Harry was *serious*. Even as half of his mind screamed that he'd be a hypocrite to ever wear that suit again, the other half was doing the math.

"So when do you want me to be here tomorrow?"

Winston asked at last, trying to sound enthusiastic. Running around in that stupid costume was the last thing he wanted to do, but he was desperate for cash. He watched, resigned, as his reinstated boss drank his straight black coffee, a satisfied expression on his slightly off-kilter face.

He knew I'd do it all along! Winston realized suddenly.

For the first time since he'd met Harry, it occurred to Winston to wonder who the "smart guy" *really* was.

Kim Aquino was fine. Elizabeth couldn't remember when she'd last felt such a sweet sense of accomplishment. She knew without a doubt that today she'd made an important, probably vital difference in somebody's life. The doctors had already treated Kim's dislocated shoulder and released her, and now Elizabeth stood watching as Ryan filled out an accident report in the mint green hospital waiting room.

Elizabeth drew her wet rescue blanket around her body more tightly, wishing that she and Ryan had remembered to bring their shoes—the cold green linoleum was making her bare feet numb. Luckily no one had forced a dry blanket on her, though. For all everyone still knew, Elizabeth was wearing a bathing suit under the wet white wool. She shivered just as Ryan looked up from his report and smiled at her—his still damp swim trunks fogging up the green vinyl chair. Elizabeth smiled back happily, knowing she and Ryan had never been closer.

Just then Captain Feehan burst in, a grim expression on his face.

"Captain Feehan!" Elizabeth exclaimed, her good mood slipping a little. They had forgotten to radio in that they were okay, she realized—half the Harbor Patrol could be out looking for them.

"Oh no. I'm so sorry," Elizabeth began. "We should have radioed—"

"Yes, you should have," the captain cut her off furiously, turning on Ryan. "If I hadn't run into a boy on the beach who'd seen you speed by in the Jeep, I could have the whole damn fleet out there right now," he snapped.

"I'm sorry," Ryan said. "We were so concerned about getting the victim to the hospital that we forgot. I know that's no excuse, but I can promise you that girl wouldn't be alive right now if it wasn't for us."

Ryan smiled proudly at Elizabeth again in a way that made her heart turn over.

"She also wouldn't have been in the water if it hadn't been for you!" Captain Feehan accused Ryan angrily. "There isn't even a No Swimming sign up on that section of beach. What were you thinking, Ryan? You can't close a beach without signs."

"But the sign *is* up!" Ryan protested. "It's right in front of the tower."

"No. It isn't," the captain said.

"It is!" Ryan insisted. "I put it up myself!"

"Are you sure?" Captain Feehan asked, looking very suspicious. He glanced questioningly from Ryan to Elizabeth and back again.

"Of course I'm sure," Ryan said.

Elizabeth couldn't believe it. They had just saved someone's life, and instead of congratulations Ryan was getting the third degree from the sheriff!

"Captain Feehan—," Elizabeth began hotly, but Ryan cut her off.

"The sign was there. I swear," he told Captain Feehan anxiously, a desperate note creeping into his voice.

Why is he getting so defensive? Elizabeth asked herself, deeply surprised. Was it possible that Ryan *had* forgotten to put up the sign? Now that she was thinking about it, Elizabeth didn't remember seeing one as she ran into the water to make the rescue. Still, at the time she'd had more important things on her mind than No Swimming signs—if Ryan said it was up, then Elizabeth was sure it must be.

She sat down beside Ryan and took his hand, squeezing it reassuringly. But Ryan's fingers remained limp, unresponsive. All traces of his earlier smiles were gone, and his expression was blank and guarded again. *If that sign isn't there,* Elizabeth worried silently, *we're all going to be in a lot of trouble.*

*　　　*　　　*

Wendy struggled through the back door, trying to balance on her shoulder the forty-pound sack of low-calorie dog food she'd just purchased. Fighting her way out of the wind and into the kitchen at last, she set the sodden bag down on the red-and-black parquet floor and took off her dripping coat.

"Paloma!" she called, expecting him to come running. But there was no sign of the dog. "That's weird," she muttered to herself as she dragged the heavy bag of food across the floor and into the pantry.

After she'd seen Winston off on his job interview, Wendy had gone to the pet store to find out what to do about her dog's little weight problem—not that Paloma was really *fat*. *This new food ought to take care of it fast,* she congratulated herself, but she was concerned that Paloma hadn't come when she'd called. She hoped no one had let him out in the storm.

He's probably just passed out on my bed and can't hear me, Wendy reassured herself, walking across the kitchen on her way to go check.

The scribbled note propped against the telephone caught her eye as she walked by:

Wendy—
Paloma's sick. We took him to the vet.
Don't worry. Back soon, Nina.

"Don't *worry!*" Wendy shrieked, terrified. Paloma was fine when she'd left just an hour before!

What could be so wrong with him now that they'd had to rush him to the vet without her?

She ran out into the living room, her heart thudding sickeningly against her rib cage. "Nina!" she shouted. "Elizabeth!"

No one answered. The house was empty except for her. Frantically Wendy ran back to the kitchen and reread Nina's note.

"It doesn't even say what vet they took him to!" she cried. What if he was *dying*? She had to find him.

Thinking quickly, Wendy climbed onto the counter and opened the high cupboard where they kept the yellow pages. How many vets could there be in Sweet Valley Shore? She'd just call down the list until she found Paloma.

She'd found the right page and was reaching to dial the first number when the phone rang by itself. Praying it was Nina, Wendy snatched it off the hook.

"Hello?" she shouted into the receiver.

"Wendy Wolman?" asked a guy's voice she didn't recognize. *Great*, she groaned to herself. She'd have to get rid of whoever it was fast—he was tying up the phone.

"Yes," she said impatiently. "Who's this?"

"My name is Monty . . . ," the caller began.

"Monty? Look, Monty, I don't know who you are or what you want, but you caught me at a really bad time. I have to go."

"Don't hang up!" Monty told her, before she could do just that. "I'm calling for Paloma."

"Thank goodness!" Wendy exclaimed, realizing that Monty must be with the vet's office. "How is he?"

"He's fine," Monty answered. He seemed a little surprised by her question, but his tone barely registered as Wendy slumped with relief.

"Where are you?" she asked more calmly, fumbling for a pencil. "I'm coming over right now. I won't be happy until I see him myself."

"You *want* to see him?" Monty asked. "But I thought . . ."

"Of *course* I want to see him," Wendy cut him off. "He's *my* dog."

There was a silence on the other end of the line.

"So give me your address," Wendy prodded.

More silence.

Then a sickening thought hit her. Maybe Paloma wasn't fine after all! Maybe they didn't *want* her to see him!

"You've got to tell me where you are," she begged, hysteria creeping into her voice. "What's the matter?"

"Uh, Wendy," Monty said at last. "I think there's some kind of mix-up. I don't know anything about a dog. I'm a concert promoter calling for Pedro Paloma. He's playing in town on Monday and he wants you to be there."

Wendy could feel the tears beginning as the back of her throat tightened. It was just too much. Her dog could be in pain or dying somewhere and now Pedro's *lackeys* were calling to bother her.

"Your timing couldn't be worse," she told Monty coldly, fighting for control. "I've got to go now."

But Monty wasn't hanging up without an answer. "So can I tell Pedro you'll be there?" he pressed. "It means a lot to him."

"No, I won't be there!" Wendy exploded. "And if you haven't figured it out, I have more important things to think about than Pedro Paloma and his stupid sympathy dates. Now leave me alone!" She slammed down the receiver, sobbing convulsively.

Chapter Six

"That was one sick puppy," Dr. Dennis told Nina and Paul, joining them on the slick orange bench in the small waiting room. "Where did he get hold of those hot dogs?"

"We don't know," Nina said, looking to Paul for confirmation. "He used to be a stray, and he still eats anything he can find. Were they bad or something?"

"I'll say," the vet agreed. "They were poisoned."

"Poisoned!" Nina gasped. Who would want to poison a big harmless sweetie like Paloma?

"I should have been watching him better," she groaned, feeling horribly guilty. "If anything had happened . . ."

"He's going to be fine," the doctor assured her. "I pumped his stomach and he's better already. We'll keep him overnight as a precaution. You can pick him up tomorrow afternoon."

"Wow," Nina said shakily as Dr. Dennis left the room. "That was close."

"Yeah," Paul agreed. His eyes were sympathetic.

"If you hadn't found him when you did . . . ," Nina began. "If we hadn't had your truck . . ."

"Don't think about it," Paul advised her gently. "Everything's okay now."

"But what if he'd *died*?" Nina asked, tears slipping down her cheeks. "It would have been my fault."

"No, it wouldn't." Paul drew her to him, his arms slipping under her bulky open jacket and closing around the smooth red fabric of her bathing suit. "It would have been the fault of the psycho who gave him those hot dogs."

After the ordeal she'd just been through, it felt good to have Paul's arms around her. Nina held on tightly, wanting to be comforted.

He's a good friend to be here for me like this, she thought, her tears of relief falling unchecked. She buried her wet face against his neck, taking in the smell of his warm skin.

"Nina," Paul whispered, his voice suddenly husky. He lowered his head and kissed a tear from her cheek.

"No!" she protested, pulling back.

"Why not?" he asked quietly, continuing to hold her. "I care about you—"

"You can't!" she interrupted, shaken and confused. "I mean, I care about you, too, but . . ."

"Then there's no problem," Paul reassured her, trying to kiss her again.

But Nina twisted free of his arms. "Yes, there is," she said, refusing to meet his eyes. "There's a big problem."

And it's getting more out of control all the time, she added to herself.

Captain Feehan was leaving the hospital waiting room as Jessica came in, supported by Ben.

Just what I need, Jessica moaned silently as she spotted Elizabeth and Ryan in the room as well.

Her head was throbbing from the blow she'd received, and she was soaked and covered with sand. She knew she looked horrific.

"Who gave you that goose egg?" Captain Feehan stopped to ask her, his curiosity aroused by the enormous purple lump on Jessica's right temple.

"You'll never believe it," Ben offered loudly before Jessica could invent a dignified explanation. "Jessica here is probably the first person in history to be knocked unconscious by a No Swimming sign. I found her near the Main Tower, facedown in the sand."

Ben laughed and the admissions clerk joined in. Apparently the thought of her predicament was so amusing, they just couldn't control themselves.

"It's not funny," Jessica snapped, not at all grateful to her rescuer—especially now that he'd embarrassed her in front of Ryan and that traitor

Elizabeth. "My new dress is completely ruined and so is my manicure. Look at this!" she demanded, crossing the room and shoving her hands under her sister's face.

Long contact with the sand had pitted and dulled the fresh red polish, and here and there grains of sand were actually cemented in. "This is all your fault," Jessica accused her twin.

"*My* fault?" Elizabeth gasped. "It is not."

"No, it's not," Captain Feehan agreed. "*Ryan* put up the No Swimming signs. Don't you know you're supposed to secure those signs with ropes?" he demanded of Ryan, as if Ryan were an idiot or a little child.

Jessica was so put out that it barely came through to her that she'd just gotten Ryan in trouble. *And so what if I did?* she thought. He certainly deserved it. *That's what he gets for fooling around with Elizabeth instead of paying attention to his job,* Jessica noted vindictively, glaring at her sister.

"What's your problem, Jess?" Elizabeth demanded, returning her angry stare.

Elizabeth was still wrapped in the same wet rescue blanket. Jessica wondered if anyone in the room besides her and Ryan knew what was under it—or, to be more precise, what wasn't. She'd wipe that smug, self-righteous look off her sister's face.

"What's *your* problem?" Jessica shot back.

"I can't wait till tomorrow, when . . ."

Jessica cut herself off right on the verge of revelation. She was so angry, she'd almost spilled her big secret.

I'm not going to call Tom after all, Jessica decided on the spot. *I'd rather let him catch her red-handed.*

Elizabeth was furious. It was nothing new for Jessica to think only of herself, but this time she'd gone too far.

Jessica thinks she's in love with Ryan, but she doesn't even care that she may have just cost him his job, Elizabeth thought, disgusted. She turned away from the emergency admittance desk, where Ben was helping Jessica fill out some forms, and focused instead on Ryan and Captain Feehan.

The two were arguing by the door in low, heated voices, but it looked to Elizabeth as if Captain Feehan was doing most of the arguing and Ryan was taking most of the heat. *Why doesn't he stand up for himself?* she wondered, biting her lip nervously to keep from butting in again.

Finally Captain Feehan finished, and Ryan turned and stalked angrily out the door without looking back. Elizabeth threw one last dirty look in Jessica's direction before she ran out after him into the storm.

"Ryan!" she called, catching up as he reached the Jeep. "What are you doing?" The rain was pouring harder than ever, and her hair was instantly plastered to her head again.

"Get in," he growled reluctantly, looking her over. "I'll take you home."

"I don't want to go home," Elizabeth protested. "I want to go back to the tower and get my clothes and . . ."

"I said I'll take you *home*," Ryan snapped, starting the engine.

Fighting tears, Elizabeth climbed in silently on the passenger's side. She'd been so close to getting through to him, and now it was all ruined. She blinked her blue-green eyes again and again as they drove through the flooded streets to her house.

"Look," Ryan said at last. "Things have to stay cool between you and me. I can't be responsible for your happiness, and I'm just not interested in hurting someone else."

"What do you mean?" Elizabeth's voice quivered.

"Just what I said," Ryan answered. "You've got a boyfriend and I've got a history. I'm not going to hurt you."

"But you're hurting me right now," Elizabeth told him, her tear-filled eyes finally spilling over.

Ryan looked at her, and for a moment they connected again.

"I'm sorry," he said sincerely, putting his hand on hers. Just for a second Elizabeth saw real pain in his expression. Then his voice iced over and his brown eyes went dead. He took his hand away.

"But this is how it's going to be," he said.

It was after midnight, but Nina couldn't sleep. There were too many thoughts running through her head: Paul, the dog, the weather. Paul . . . and now Jessica had a big lump on her head and was excused from duty on Sunday. If the rain cleared up, they'd be short a much needed lifeguard.

"This is ridiculous," Nina muttered to herself, throwing aside the covers. Taking her weather radio from the nightstand, she opened her bedroom door and crept down the stairs to the living room. If she couldn't sleep, at least she could listen to the weather reports. She was standing at the front window, listening to the radio and watching the rain, when the back door slammed.

Her heart started pounding wildly. Everyone else was asleep—what if it was a prowler? What if it was the person who'd poisoned Paloma? Should she scream?

She heard heavy footsteps walking down the hall and Ben stormed into the room. He was soaked and furious, and held a flashlight in his hand.

"You're up!" he said loudly, looking surprised.

"I'm surprised the whole house isn't up after the way you just slammed the door," Nina fired back in an annoyed stage whisper. "Did it ever occur to you that you might scare someone?"

"I'm sorry," he apologized, lowering his voice a little, "but you won't believe what I just found out."

"What?" she whispered, motioning for him to follow her into the kitchen. They could talk there with less fear of waking the others.

"Someone cut the ropes on the No Swimming sign that hit Jessica. When I found her lying there unconscious, I never thought to look. But later, at the hospital, Captain Feehan and Ryan were fighting about whether or not Ryan had secured the sign. The more I thought about it, the more it started to bug me. I couldn't sleep anyway, so I figured I might as well go check."

Ben sat at the kitchen table while Nina filled a kettle with water for hot chocolate. "*Love* the lingerie, by the way," he informed her from behind.

Nina blushed as she realized what she was wearing: a long, red flannel granny gown with little black-and-white cows all over it and a pair of thick white sweat socks. It had seemed like a good choice for such miserable weather, but it wasn't exactly fantasy material. Leave it to Ben to point it out.

"Glad you like it," she said smoothly, sitting down across from him. "Maybe I'll let you borrow it sometime."

"Only if it comes with the socks," he teased before returning to his main subject.

"Seriously, Nina," he said, suddenly frowning. "I think someone is out to get us."

"What?" Nina said, not wanting to admit that the same sickening thought had occurred to her too. First someone had poisoned Wendy's dog, and now it seemed as if someone had cut down their No Swimming sign.

"Who would want to get us?" she objected. "It doesn't make sense."

"It makes perfect sense," Ben said. "It's got to be the South Beach Squad. They want us to look bad so they'll earn all the merit pay this summer."

"You can't be serious. I know they want to beat us, but they wouldn't stoop so low as to poison a *dog*!"

"You have no idea how low Rachel will stoop," Ben said grimly. "She's the greediest little witch I've ever met. It's like money's a disease with her or something."

"But it's pointless," Nina protested. "How does poisoning Wendy's dog help Rachel's squad to beat us?"

"I don't know," Ben admitted, "unless she's trying to scare us and get us fighting among ourselves. But what about the No Swimming sign? That's a different story—that sign could have gotten Ryan fired."

He was right, of course, and Nina grimaced as she considered the consequences. If Ryan was off the squad, they'd lose their leader and disintegrate into a fifth-rate team that South Beach could beat easily. They'd lose the merit-pay contest for sure, and more important, lives would be at risk.

"The question is," Ben said, "who's doing Rachel's dirty work?"

"What do you mean?" Nina asked. The kettle started to screech and she jumped to snatch it from the burner before it could wake the others.

"I mean, Rachel never works alone," Ben explained as Nina opened the packets of hot chocolate and added the boiling water. "She's a total melodrama junkie. It's no fun for her to cause a scene unless she can hurt at least ten people in the process. That's her specialty, in fact—turning people against each other and dragging them along with her instead."

"Nice girl." Nina sat down with the two mugs of chocolate. "I can see why you broke up with her."

"I wish I'd never gone out with her! But that doesn't answer my question. Who cut down that sign?"

"Oh no," Nina said quietly, a horrible thought occurring to her. She tried to shake it off, but it wouldn't go away. "No," she whispered, "it can't be."

"What can't be?" Ben asked intently. "What are you thinking?"

"It's nothing," she said, not wanting to believe her own suspicions. "It's just that . . . well . . . Paul Jackson is joining the South Beach Squad tomorrow, and I saw him earlier today with a big knife.

And he was the one who found Paloma, too—right in the nick of time. Oh no—it *can't* be."

"Don't be so sure," Ben said quietly. "Rachel can be *very* persuasive. She has a way of making sure her guys aren't thinking with their heads, if you know what I mean."

"But why would Paul poison the dog and then rescue it?" Nina demanded, trying hard not to picture Paul with Rachel. "It doesn't make sense. And why would a lifeguard risk lives? Paul's not like that."

"He probably *wasn't* like that," Ben agreed, "but if he's with Rachel now, all bets are off."

"I don't believe it."

"You don't have to believe it," Ben told her. "Just pay attention—that's all I'm saying. *Everyone* on the South Beach Squad is a suspect now."

"You're right," Nina agreed slowly, reluctantly.

"If they manage to get Ryan fired . . ." Ben let the sentence trail off.

"I know," Nina said. It was too horrible to even think about.

"Ryan is the best lifeguard I've ever met. I'd rather work under him than anyone. In spite of his problems."

"What problems?" Nina asked, surprised.

Ben shrugged. "Rachel told me what happened last summer. *You* know. Ryan's little habit of—"

"Oh, that," Nina interrupted quickly, begging him with her eyes not to say it out loud.

"It's true, then?" Ben searched her face.

"It's true," Nina confirmed, dropping her gaze. "But do me a favor—keep it to yourself."

She didn't even want to think about *that* right now.

Chapter Seven

"Rise and shine, people!" Nina's voice echoed loudly down the halls of the three-story house. "It is absolutely *gorgeous* outside!"

Wendy heard Nina through the tail end of a dream. Between her scare over Paloma Perro and her tears over Pedro Paloma, she'd passed a terrible, all but sleepless night.

"Just a few more minutes," Wendy murmured, still half unconscious.

Boom, boom, boom!

"Up and at 'em, Wendy!" Nina shouted, pounding on Wendy's bedroom door. "It's going to be *busy* at the beach today!"

The adrenaline that jolted through Wendy's body at the sudden, unexpected racket almost made her retch. If Nina hadn't been responsible for saving her dog's life the night before, Wendy might have felt the need to retaliate. As it was, she figured she ought to forgive Nina just about anything.

"I'm up," she yelled grouchily, wishing she weren't.

But once Wendy saw the unexpected sunlight streaming through the open slats of her mini-blinds, she felt better. She got out of bed, crossed to the window, and drew the blinds up to the very top.

Nina was right—the weather *was* gorgeous. Wendy could barely believe that the beautiful sunny beach outside her window this morning was part of the same ugly gray stretch of sand she'd worked the day before. It was still practically dawn, but already the beach umbrellas and towels were being laid out as people tried to cordon off space for friends coming down later. The surf was larger than usual, Wendy noted, and the water would probably stay that muddy, stirred-up shade of green for a week, but everything considered, it was an unbelievably beautiful day.

Wendy suddenly felt good. Maybe things in her life weren't going that great, but they weren't going that badly, either. She'd spoken to the vet after Nina had returned and found out that Paloma was fine—she could pick him up on her lunch break. Not only that, but Winston had finally found a job! She was so happy for him—even happier because she'd been able to help. *Not bad,* she congratulated herself once again. *He never even suspected I made up that assistant manager thing.*

Her plans for Winston had certainly worked out better than Winston's plans for her. She wished she'd never *told* him about her crush on Pedro Paloma. She didn't even know which of them she was madder at anymore.

She threw open her tiny attic window and took a few deep breaths of the cleansing, early morning air.

Pedro, she decided. *I'm definitely madder at Pedro.*

And who needed him anyway? She had her dog, she had her job, and she had some really great friends. What more could a girl ask for?

Wendy smiled as she pulled on her red lifeguard suit. The Sweet Valley Shore Squad was going to save some major butt today.

Jessica stood in front of her dresser mirror, checking the goose egg on her temple. It was still pretty ugly, but not quite as bad as the day before. She'd iced it all night to bring the swelling down, but although it was smaller, it was definitely a darker shade of purple now.

Gross! she thought, annoyed. She prodded it gently and winced at the unexpected pain. *This is all Elizabeth's fault. I swear I'll get her back—*

Jessica stopped in mid-thought, and a satisfied smile spread slowly across her tan features. As it turned out, revenge was only a couple of hours away. Tom was coming today.

Jessica returned her attention to the mirror and studied the lump on her head more carefully. She was pretty sure now that a good makeup job would hide it. *Besides,* she thought, *it got me out of work today!* She didn't have a concussion and would have to work on the Fourth, but for today she was a free woman. She couldn't wait for Isabella to arrive with Danny and Tom.

Pulling on a yellow polka-dot sundress, Jessica headed down the stairs. This would be a great day. After she'd sent everyone else off to work, she'd lie out in her bikini for an hour or two and work on her tan. Then she'd go into town and get another dress for the rave at the cannery that night. If she played her cards right, there might even be time to get her nails redone. . . .

Jessica's steps slowed as she walked past Elizabeth's open door. Her twin was primping in front of the full-length mirror, inching up her lifeguard suit to make it more revealing. *So very un-Liz-like.* Jessica smiled to herself. *And such a waste of effort.*

If her sister only knew. By this time tomorrow, Ryan would be all Jessica's.

For the first time in weeks Winston had a more compelling reason to get out of bed than hurrying to the kitchen before Ben hogged all the Froot

Loops. Today his life had meaning, purpose—today he was going to work!

Winston bounded off his mattress and hurriedly pulled on some oversized shorts and a white T-shirt. Nina was still running all over the house acting like a drill sergeant, but Winston didn't mind. It was a gorgeous, *beautiful* day, and he finally had something better to do than watch cartoons. Not only that, he was going to get paid! In beautiful, glorious cash.

All right, so he was going to be a human hamburger. But what did it matter? He was finally going to make some money.

Besides, this is the kind of job I can really sink my teeth into, Winston told himself—the first of what he knew for sure would become an enormously long string of bad puns.

"Eat at Hamburger Harry's," he told his reflection in the mirror over the dresser, flashing his goofiest practice grin. "Uh-huh-huh-huh," he giggled dementedly.

What the heck. If it was his destiny to be a hamburger, then he'd be the best darn hamburger the boardwalk had ever seen.

It had seemed to Nina as if she just couldn't get to the beach fast enough. The entire time she was getting ready for work, a steady stream of cars had been making its way past the house and down to the beach parking areas. By eight A.M., when the squad finally assembled in front of the Main Tower, the sand was surprisingly crowded. Nina noted with relief that Marcus, Paula, and Kerry were already there with Ryan as she sprinted across the beach to join them, her housemates right behind her.

All but Jessica, of course. Nina could *almost* believe that Jessica had given herself that lump on purpose just to get out of working.

Ryan made the work assignments, and Nina drew the South Tower with Kerry Janowitz. Normally she would have protested that decision—the South Tower didn't usually see much action—but today she was glad. Working there would give her an opportunity to keep an eye on the adjacent South Beach Squad. Besides, the whole beach was bound to be a zoo today— there'd be plenty of action for everyone.

"It's going to be a hot one," Kerry observed as they trudged down the sand to their tower.

Nina smiled at her tall, red-headed companion. Kerry was thin, but incredibly strong and capable—Nina always enjoyed working with him.

"You said it," Nina agreed. "Not *too* hot, I hope."

Kerry nodded his understanding of Nina's double meaning. "We can handle it," he said confidently.

I hope so, Nina worried, looking around at the growing crowds. Normally she would have shared or even surpassed Kerry's confidence, but not after last night. She and Ben had agreed to keep their suspicions to themselves, to keep from worrying the others, but now Nina wondered if that had been smart. Maybe it would have been better to warn everyone to watch out for foul play.

As she climbed the steps to her tower Nina noticed some teenagers to the south who were getting pretty rowdy, and the group of adults they had come with was already into the beer. The day was sure to be a major challenge. *If only I didn't have to worry about sabotage on top of everything else,* she thought, opening and securing the window boards distractedly.

"Uh, Nina? Are you okay?" Kerry asked from his position at the rail.

"Of course," Nina answered, surprised. "Why do you ask?"

"No reason," Kerry said quickly, keeping his eyes out to sea and his back to the tower.

Nina realized that she had her own back to the water—one of the worst mistakes a lifeguard could make. Not only that, she hadn't glanced at the ocean once since she'd climbed the tower stairs. It was a total beginner's error.

Ben and I made the right decision after all, Nina decided on the spot. *Let the others concentrate on their jobs.*

"So what do you think?" Ryan asked, lowering his binoculars.

"It looks like a great day," Elizabeth answered happily. She still couldn't believe that Ryan had chosen *her* to work the Main Tower with him instead of Nina. It made good sense, of course, to spread out the squad's two best guards on such a busy day, but Ryan had never picked Elizabeth for his tower partner before.

"I mean, what do you think about the surf?" he clarified in his usual no-nonsense manner. "It's still a storm swell."

If he didn't share Elizabeth's *total* enthusiasm for their unusual togetherness, at least he was being nice to her again. Elizabeth resolved not to let his I-am-a-detached-professional act get her down this time.

"It's pretty big," she acknowledged, "but not out of control."

"I don't like it," he said. "It's too confused—the currents are still too strong. Why don't you take the Jeep and go tell everyone to put out the red flags? I'll hold down the station while you're gone."

"You're the boss," Elizabeth said cheerfully, grabbing the Jeep keys off the peg inside the door.

The weather was perfect and the beach was so beautiful that Elizabeth couldn't help wondering if Ryan had sent her out in the Jeep just to let her enjoy herself. *Ryan would never do that,* she told herself immediately, sure that she was right. Even so, it was undeniably cool to be driving along the hard-packed wet sand in the bright red Jeep. And her being a lifeguard wasn't keeping the guys from checking her out, either.

"Marry me!" an especially cute African American guy in green swim trunks called to her, dropping to his knees in the sand.

Elizabeth smiled at him flirtatiously and tossed her long hair before she realized she was acting exactly like Jessica. The thought froze the smile on her face. For the rest of the trip down the beach Elizabeth resolved to stick to business.

The sand and surf were alive with both locals and tourists, and the scene was as wild and colorful as anything she'd ever seen. *A few of those sunburns are going to be pretty colorful too,* she said to herself, spotting a group that was probably seeing its first palm trees. There were surfboards and body boards and inflatable boats and beach towels and sand toys of every description strewn across the sand. *There's just nothing to compare with a Fourth of July weekend on a California beach,* Elizabeth thought, smiling again.

She reached Tower 2—Ben and Paula McFee—and veered up onto the dry sand to shout up from the Jeep, "Ryan says to put out the red flag."

Ben nodded his acknowledgment as Paula ducked inside to get the red flag—the one that notified swimmers to use extreme caution. Elizabeth waved and drove off to Tower 3, where Marcus Collier and Wendy were on guard.

"Red flags," Elizabeth yelled up to her two fellow guards. The flags were brought out and Elizabeth continued on to the south and final tower.

"Hey, Nina!" Elizabeth yelled up. "Ryan says red flags."

"Yeah," Nina said, never taking her eyes off the water. "I was just thinking that myself."

Kerry went into the tower to get the red flag.

"So how's it going?" Elizabeth asked.

"Scary! We've got tourists all over the place out here. I'll bet we make fifty rescues today."

"Optimist," Elizabeth teased.

Nina smiled. "Don't you have a job to do?"

"I'm going. I'm going." Elizabeth laughed, turning the Jeep around and heading back to her station.

"Private Wakefield reporting for duty, Chief," Elizabeth joked as she resumed her position next to Ryan at the Main Tower.

Was it possible? Did he actually *smile* a little? On *duty*?

"You're in a good mood," he observed.

"Yeah," she agreed effusively. "Why not? It's a gorgeous day, I saved a life yesterday, I'm here with the best-looking guy I know. . . ."

"Elizabeth!" Ryan stopped her, clearly taken aback.

Elizabeth was actually pretty shocked herself, but she plunged ahead anyway.

"Ryan, this is so stupid!" she exclaimed. "Why

do we have to keep pretending we don't like each other?"

He stood at the rail, staring out to sea for a full minute before he answered, even then not taking his eyes off the water.

"Look, Elizabeth," he said at last. "I think you know how I feel about you, but this thing between us can't happen. So why do you keep pretending that it can?"

"But *why* can't it?" Elizabeth asked.

"Well, you have a boyfriend, for one thing," Ryan answered.

"Yeah. See, that's the part I already know," Elizabeth replied. "How about telling me the rest this time?"

"The rest isn't important," Ryan said, closing off his face again.

"Ryan!" Elizabeth insisted

"I've got a lot to prove out here, Elizabeth. All right? You don't know what's going on with me, with my past. . . ."

"Because you won't tell me!"

He smiled reluctantly. "Are you always this stubborn?" he asked.

"I prefer to think of it as single-minded," she informed him. "And yes. Always."

"Something happened last summer," he admitted finally in a sad, bitter tone, "that totally blew my reputation—not to mention my own high opinion of my greatness. It's actually pretty astonishing that

111

I'm even still allowed to lifeguard, let alone head up the squad. I have to stay on top of *everything* this year, Elizabeth. Every second. This is my last chance."

"Tell me what happened," Elizabeth prompted.

But Ryan had apparently had enough soul baring for one morning. "Don't ask me that and I won't grill you about Tom Watts," he said.

"What do you mean?" she asked, feeling suddenly uncomfortable. It would be easier to believe she wasn't doing anything wrong if Ryan would quit mentioning Tom.

"You know what I mean," Ryan said. "The first date, the first kiss. The first time."

He turned from the rail just long enough to raise his eyebrows suggestively, and Elizabeth could feel her cheeks flushing a brilliant shade of pink. She wasn't exactly in the mood to tell a sophisticated older guy like Ryan that there'd never *been* a first time—not with Tom or anyone else. She was still trying to think of something to say when Ryan spoke again.

"So can I take you to the rave tonight?" he asked. "Or would that be too weird?"

"What?" Elizabeth gasped, taken totally by surprise. *Now* he wanted to ask her out?

"You were right." He shrugged. "All this pretending *is* getting stupid. What do you say we hang it up and just be friends?"

Chapter Eight

"I'll get him," Marcus offered.

Wendy looked hard at the surf, at the dark-haired guy thrashing around just behind the wave line as if he were having some kind of fit.

"No," she declined. "It's my save." Grabbing her orange buoy, she quickly descended the tower, never taking her eyes off the man in the water. Her feet hit the sand and she began running toward him.

It had been a long day. She and Marcus had been trading off rescues since eight that morning, although things hadn't really heated up until about eleven. It was three o'clock now, and the only time off she'd had was an incredibly rushed trip to the vet to pick up Paloma and take him back to the house—her so-called lunch break. As Wendy reached the water and began plunging through the surf toward her victim, she half wished she'd accepted Marcus's offer. She was exhausted. She hoped this guy wouldn't struggle.

Wendy cut through the water toward the victim with practiced, efficient strokes, her rescue buoy trailing out behind her. In less than a minute she was approaching her target, who had now flailed his way around so his back was to the beach and to her. It was a good position, and Wendy considered just grabbing him in a chin hold before he had a chance to see her, but it was too dangerous. If he panicked, he could drag them both under.

"It's okay," she yelled at the back of the guy's head as she pulled the buoy from behind her and pushed it out across the surface in his direction. "I'm a lifeguard, and I'm here to help you. You need to stay calm and take hold of the flotation device. I'll tow you in."

Immediately the guy stopped writhing and turned to face her. "Hi, Wendy," he said calmly.

It was Pedro Paloma.

"Pedro!" Wendy exclaimed in shock. "What are you *doing*?"

Pedro's incredibly handsome Latin face immediately assumed a foolish expression.

"You wouldn't take my calls," he explained.

"You're not drowning," Wendy accused angrily. She could see he was treading water perfectly capably. "Do you know how stupid this little stunt was?" she demanded. "Someone out here could really need me."

"*I* need you," Pedro said.

Wendy turned furiously and began to swim back toward the beach.

How dare he do this to me? What an egotistical jerk! she thought as she kicked. Then a hand closed around her ankle, stopping her forward progress. She turned quickly, violently throwing off his grip.

"What!" she snapped hotly. "What do you want?"

"I want you to go out with me."

"You're insane!" she said, outraged. "I told you I've got a job to do here. Now leave me alone!"

"Wendy, please!" Pedro begged. "I was such an idiot. I think about you constantly. Please, I have to see you."

Wendy was still furious, but Pedro looked so desperate and so sincere, dog paddling beside her in the surf, that she felt herself softening in spite of her firm resolve never to speak to him again.

"You're right about one thing—you *are* an idiot," she told him. But she didn't turn around and start swimming again like she knew she should.

"A *total* idiot!" he agreed enthusiastically. "Can you ever forgive me? Please?"

He smiled, and her traitor heart immediately caved. It was easy to hate him when she didn't have to see him, but it was a lot harder to be mad to his gorgeous face. Drops of water sparkled like crystal in his long black hair and lashes, and his dazzling white smile stood out brilliantly against the tan of his cheeks. He took her breath away.

"I forgive you," Wendy said reluctantly. "But now I have to go in."

She had just regained the sand and was squeezing the water out of her long hair when he appeared again at her side.

"So what are you doing tonight?" he asked. "Can I take you out to dinner?"

"No," she said emphatically, walking toward the tower.

"But why not?" he asked. "I thought we were friends again."

"I said I forgive you," Wendy told him. "I still never want to see you again."

He put a restraining hand on her shoulder, but she immediately spun around, shaking it off.

"I have to work!" she reminded him angrily.

"I'm sorry," he apologized. "I really am—for *everything*. Please, Wendy. Don't do this. Let me take you to dinner tonight."

"I'm going to a party with my friends," she said. "Now go away."

But he didn't go away. Instead he trailed her all the way to the tower stairs like a lost little puppy.

"Can I take you to the party?" he asked.

"No!" she shouted, amazed by his persistence. It was ridiculous. Pedro Paloma was a total

116

heartthrob. He was also sure to be famous in the very near future. Wendy could barely believe he'd waste both their time this way.

Maybe he really does care, she thought suddenly, her pulse quickening at the possibility.

No! she answered herself harshly. The two of them made a ludicrous couple. She wasn't going to let him hurt her again.

"The line on this rescue buoy is getting frayed," Nina told Kerry. "I'm going down to the storage room for a spare."

Kerry nodded his acknowledgment as Nina descended the stairs, the key to the storage closet at the tower base already in her hand. But when she turned the corner, Nina stopped short. The closet door was standing wide open.

That's weird, Nina thought, immediately on her guard. The closet was at the back of the tower, in a place not visible from the tower platform, but Nina was sure it had been closed in the morning when she and Kerry had come on duty. It was *supposed* to be closed at all times.

Nina approached the open door cautiously, wild thoughts racing through her head. Someone from the South Beach Squad could have sneaked up behind them pretty easily and gotten into the closet—all the locks used the same key. But *why?* Tiptoeing across the sand, Nina stuck her head just barely around the edge of the open door and looked inside. Her heart sank at what she saw—it was Paul, rifling through their equipment.

How could I have been so wrong about him? Nina wailed silently. It almost broke her heart to think he was involved with this. Still, she knew what she had to do.

"What are you doing?" Nina demanded sharply, stepping into the doorway.

Paul looked up casually and flashed his killer smile, as if nothing in the world was wrong. He was wearing red lifeguard trunks, and the whistle that hung from his neck only emphasized his powerful shoulders and tight waist.

"Hey, Nina," he greeted her. "What's up?"

"That's what I'd like to know. What are you doing?"

"Our red flags are trashed," Paul explained, "and Rachel wants to put them out now. I'm looking for your spare set."

"What about *your* spare set?" Nina snapped, her hands on her hips.

Paul finally seemed to notice her mood. "Jeez, calm down," he said. "I'm just borrowing them— you'll get them back. Besides, you guys have been on red all day, so it's not like you need them."

"You'd have been on red too if Rachel had any sense," Nina shot back. "And I don't appreciate you just taking whatever you want from our gear without asking. This isn't a convenience store."

"Okay, okay," Paul said, holding up his hands

for peace. "I'm sorry. I'll ask next time, all right?"

Nina stared suspiciously into his open, friendly face, trying to discern his hidden motives. But she didn't see any. All she saw was a great-looking fellow lifeguard searching for a spare set of flags.

"They're over there by the wall," she said grudgingly, pointing.

"*Thank* you." He smiled.

Paul grabbed the small canvas sack of flags and stepped out of the closet into the sunshine. Nina immediately locked the door behind him.

"Don't worry," Paul told her, misinterpreting her attitude. "The Fourth of July is always hairy. Tomorrow will be even worse, and then it will all be over—at least until Labor Day."

"I'm not a rookie," Nina reminded him icily.

Paul looked genuinely surprised by her tone.

"I didn't say you were," he said. "Is something the matter? I mean, are you mad at me or something?" He reached out and took her by the wrist, drawing her closer. "I would hate to have you mad at me," he said teasingly, searching her eyes.

"I'm not mad at you," Nina replied weakly.

"What, then?" Paul pressed.

"It's just . . . nothing."

She couldn't tell him. Even if he wasn't personally involved in the attacks on the Sweet Valley Squad, he was part of Rachel's group now.

"Will you go to the rave with me tonight?" Paul asked, still watching her intently.

"I guess so," Nina accepted uncertainly.

"Great," he said, all smiles again. "I'll pick you up at eight."

What are you doing? Nina berated herself as she climbed back up the tower stairs. *What about Bryan?*

Her eyes followed Paul's broad back as he trudged through the sand to rejoin the South Beach Squad, and she felt an incredible surge of longing. What would it be like to run her hands over his perfect, coffee-with-cream-colored skin?

Stop it! she ordered herself immediately. For all she knew, Paul was the enemy. And *she* had a boyfriend.

Oh no, she thought unhappily, wishing she'd turned Paul down. *What am I getting into?*

The boardwalk was packed, and Winston was having the time of his life.

"Will you look at that kid?" Winston heard an old guy tell his wife. "He's hilarious."

"Eat at Hamburger Harry's," Winston advised them, and they smiled.

Winston felt like a king—King of the Boardwalk. He was really making people's day *and* he was having a great time doing it. Not only that, Harry's place was doing incredible business. Winston knew, because he'd eaten lunch there himself—on the house. Harry was absolutely stoked with him.

Then, out of nowhere, things took a turn for the worse.

"Get off my boardwalk, you obnoxious little weenie," rasped a hostile voice behind him.

Winston turned to find himself face-to-face with his new arch-nemesis—Hot Dog Howie.

"It takes one to know one," Winston retorted, eyeing the giant human hot dog.

"Yeah?" snarled Howie loudly. "Well, I've had just about enough of you cutting into my action. Now get your pathetic, saggy buns off my boardwalk!"

There was a wave of appreciative snickering from the people within earshot, and a crowd started to form.

Winston was shocked. Of course, he hadn't expected Howie to *enjoy* having competition, but Winston had as much right to be on the boardwalk as the next person.

"Who's going to make me?" Winston asked, trying to sound manly and dangerous. "You?"

As soon as he said it, he wished he hadn't. Winston was younger and taller than the hot-dog vendor, but Howie had a big weight advantage. Not only that, he looked pretty mean.

Howie glanced around the crowd, stalling for effect. "I could," he rasped lazily, "but we've got kids on this boardwalk who get *paid* to pick up the trash."

The crowd roared with laughter as Winston

struggled unsuccessfully to think of a witty come-back. It was humiliating. A minute ago everyone had been laughing *with* him. Now they were laughing *at* him.

"You take that back!" Winston demanded shakily.

"Not a chance," Howie said, his tone insulting.

The crowd immediately began to chant: "Fight, fight, fight!"

The next thing Winston knew, he had launched himself furiously at Hot Dog Howie, grabbing him in a sort of giant bear hug and trying to take him to the ground. Howie wasn't going out easy, though. He struggled, grabbing Winston's back bun with both hands and holding on tight. The two giant meals-on-legs wrestled ferociously in their cumbersome costumes, each trying to trip the other, but they couldn't get close enough to do any real damage. It was more like a bizarre form of dancing than fighting.

"Fifteen bucks on the hot dog!" a man yelled suddenly from the growing crowd. "Fifteen bucks says the hamburger hits the deck first."

"You're on!" someone accepted immediately. Out of the corner of his eye Winston saw the guy whip a twenty out of his pocket and wave it in the air.

"Ten on the hamburger!" someone else yelled. Several takers responded instantly.

"You're finished now, burger boy," Howie

snarled as he got hold of the lettuce around Winston's neck and tried to drag him down.

"I don't think so, you big . . . fat . . . *wiener!*" Winston panted in reply as his hand encountered the center crack at the back of Howie's buns.

The crowd erupted in laughter and the betting escalated. Wagers were being screamed out all over the place.

"A hundred dollars on the wiener!" someone yelled.

Winston and Howie both stopped struggling, momentarily stunned. A hush fell over the startled crowd too, but only for a second.

"You're on!" someone else yelled, covering the action.

Winston's eyes met Howie's, and suddenly it was as if they were reading each other's minds.

"I've had just about enough of you!" Winston yelled, pretending to resume the fight. He gripped his opponent tightly, bringing his mouth in close to Howie's ear.

"Are you thinking what I'm thinking?" Winston whispered.

"Yeah," Howie grunted under his breath.

"On the count of three," Winston said. "One, two, three."

The two titans shoved away from each other violently and went reeling backward into the crowd. Only a wall of people pressing in around them kept them from falling.

"You call that fighting, you foot-long weakling?" Winston taunted, stepping forward.

"Oh, yeah? Well, at least I'm a foot long," Howie shot back. "Maybe we can find *you* a Vienna sausage suit." He glanced insultingly in the direction of Winston's midsection.

"I could take you with one tomato tied behind my back," Winston shouted in angry reply.

"In your dreams," snarled Howie, giving Winston a shove.

"That's it," Winston roared, pointing at Howie. "You be here tomorrow—same time, same place. Your leathery old buns are going to hit the boardwalk so hard they'll need surgery."

"I'll be here," Howie assured him.

Winston heard the crowd groan with disappointment as people put away their wallets. But he heard something else, too—excitement. They'd be back.

Winston smiled as he pushed away from his rival and strutted down the boardwalk. He and Howie were going to make a lot of money.

Jessica flipped through the pages of her newest magazine one last time before she tossed it distractedly onto the cranberry-and-white-striped sofa beside her. It was four o'clock, and Isabella and the guys should have arrived hours before. Jessica had had more than enough time to tan her stomach, buy a new dress, have her nails done, *and* get totally bored.

"Where *are* they?" she asked herself impatiently, speaking out loud.

"Here we are!" Jessica took a quick step toward the door, then sighed in exasperation as she realized it was only Ben with two of his female admirers.

"I didn't mean *you*," she sulked, turning her back on him.

"The bathroom's that way, girls," Ben said behind her. Jessica could hear the two tittering groupies she'd just glimpsed head off in the direction Ben had indicated.

"If you weren't waiting for me, then who?" Ben asked, dropping his sweaty, sandy body onto the sofa beside her.

All he was wearing was his lifeguard suit, and it was on the tip of Jessica's tongue to say something rude. Maybe something about the fact that his unwashed body shouldn't be on the furniture, or perhaps a dig about the Airhead Patrol in the bathroom. She tossed her long blond hair and opened her mouth to put him in his place, but nothing came out.

The truth was, he looked incredibly sexy. Tan and lean, with just a dusting of sand in his black chest hair and across those washboard abs. She had to admit he even smelled kind of good. Sweaty, yes, but salty too, and like the coconut sunscreen that glistened on his strong, tan shoulders.

"So how are you feeling today?" he asked her seriously, abandoning his fooling around.

"Fine," she answered, momentarily confused.

Ben reached out and stroked the bump on her temple so gently it was almost a caress. It was very . . . sensual. Jessica felt herself flushing as she realized for the first time how mean she'd been to him the night before. Ben had come out to find her in the middle of a hurricane and she hadn't said a single nice thing.

"Uh, thanks for taking me to the hospital," she told him shyly.

"No problem," he said, letting his hand drop from her face and trail slowly along her bare arm. "I can't think of anyone I'd rather go to the hospital with."

Jessica was getting flustered. "Yeah. Well, thanks," she said.

"If you *really* want to thank me," Ben suggested, "go to the rave with me tonight."

There he went again! It was just like Ben to ask her out when he knew she'd say no. He always had to ruin everything.

"You know I'm interested in someone else," Jessica said, annoyed.

Ben sat up as if he'd been stung. "Why, of *course* you are," he agreed sarcastically. "The studly Ryan Taylor—how could I have forgotten?"

"Beats me," Jessica retorted in self-defense. "Maybe you're stupid."

"They don't let stupid people in Mensa," Ben countered angrily.

"There are all different kinds of stupid," she informed him.

"Well, I'll have to bow to your greater expertise on the subject," Ben said. "I'm sure you know more about stupidity than I *ever* will."

Jessica was still glaring him down, trying to think of an adequate comeback, when the Gruesome Twosome came giggling back from the bathroom.

"Oh, Ben," the blond in the black bikini said, "we just *love* your house!"

"It's absolutely *precious!*" her friend in the neon green thong bathing suit agreed, sidling up next to him.

It was all Jessica could do not to vomit.

"Don't you have somewhere to go?" She gave him the most evil look she could manage.

"As a matter of fact, I do," Ben answered in a voice so cold it felt like an early winter. Then he turned his back on her.

"Break time's over, ladies," he announced pleasantly to the oblivious girls who had followed him home. "And I've got to get back to my tower. Just let me grab a snack."

There was an awkward silence between the three girls left behind in the living room as Ben pushed through the swinging door into the kitchen. Mercifully it was only a few seconds before he came back out, a banana gripped in each hand.

Like pistols, Jessica thought instantly, a sense of déjà vu causing the flesh on the back of her neck to prickle. *Or something I saw once in a dream.* He looked up, and their eyes locked and held.

"Paloma's sleeping in the kitchen," he told her curtly. "Make sure you keep an eye on him."

But Jessica barely heard Ben's instructions. He was still walking toward her with the bananas, and she was trying to shake off the inexplicably eerie feeling that seeing him that way gave her, when a car horn suddenly blared outside.

"Finally!" Jessica exclaimed, leaping off the sofa and smoothing the skirt of her yellow sundress.

"Finally what?" Ben asked, but Jessica was already running past him out the door, rushing to greet her company.

"Izzy!" Jessica squealed, hugging her friend enthusiastically. "I'm so glad to see you! Where have you *been?*"

Isabella rolled her beautiful gray eyes and lifted her long dark hair off her neck.

"Well, first of all *someone* couldn't get up this morning," she said. A meaningful glance in her boyfriend, Danny Wyatt's, direction let Jessica know who the "someone" was. "And by the time we got going, we were stuck in the traffic of the century. So then *someone* thought we might as well pull over and have lunch. The next thing I knew we were stuck in this horrible dive with the worst service I've ever seen for, like, an hour."

"It wasn't that long!" Danny protested, appealing to his best friend for support. "Back me up here, Tom."

"Sorry, man." Tom Watts smiled, shaking his head. "It felt more like *two* hours to me." He ran a hand through his windblown brown hair, trying to untangle it. Tom looked good, Jessica noted with satisfaction. He would have to change out of that sweaty T-shirt, of course, but he was unexpectedly tan and his dark eyes flashed with good humor.

"How awful," Jessica sympathized, taking Isabella's backpack and looking eagerly around for something else to carry. The entire backseat was crammed so full of knapsacks and sleeping bags and groceries that Jessica barely knew where to start.

"Oh, it gets worse," Danny volunteered, stepping forward. The mint green polo shirt he wore looked great against his dark brown skin, but it was dirty and soaked with sweat. "*Someone* hadn't had her car serviced for, like, a hundred years, and we blew a radiator hose on the freeway about a mile from the nearest exit."

"Oh no." Jessica couldn't help giggling at Danny's dead accurate imitation of his girl-friend.

"It was your basic nightmare," Isabella acknowledged, stretching her bare arms overhead. Her pink tank top was damp and rumpled, and her white walking shorts were so wrinkled they looked like she'd put them on the week before. "Thank goodness we're finally here! It's so much *cooler* here than at campus. It feels like heaven just to . . ."

Isabella trailed off, apparently distracted by something in the yard. "Hello," she said suddenly, holding out her hand. "I'm Isabella Ricci."

"Yes, you are," Ben agreed, smiling flirtatiously and taking the hand she'd extended. Isabella seemed charmed, but Jessica was disgusted. She hated it when Ben smiled at women that way—did he really believe it had any effect?

"And this is my boyfriend, Danny Wyatt," Isabella continued. "And Elizabeth's boyfriend, Tom Watts."

"How's it going?" Ben greeted them, nodding in their direction. "And how interesting to finally meet *you*, Tom," he added, looking pointedly from Tom to Jessica. "Elizabeth's told us all about you, but she never mentioned you were visiting today."

"It's a surprise," Jessica cut in quickly, wishing Ben would mind his own business. "Come on," she urged her friends. "Let's get all this stuff inside, and you can change clothes if you want to.

Then we'll walk into town and I'll show you around."

"Can we go say hi to Elizabeth?" Tom asked. "I can't wait to see her."

"Of course," Jessica said smoothly, pretending not to notice Ben's suspicious, disapproving stares. "That'll be fun."

For an idiot, Ben was too darn smart.

Chapter Nine

Elizabeth sighed happily as she pushed through the dresses on the rack. Ryan had let half the squad go home at five, when the crowds had thinned out, and Elizabeth had rushed straight to town to buy something new before the boutiques closed up. She wanted to wear something special for her date with Ryan—something that he would remember.

He'll remember this! Elizabeth thought, holding up a very skimpy red minidress, but she already knew that it wasn't her style. *Jessica could get away with it—maybe,* she thought.

Comparing her behavior to Jessica's was becoming a regular thing with her lately, Elizabeth noted, heaving another, far less happy sigh. It wasn't that Elizabeth didn't love her sister; she just didn't want to *be* her sister.

It's this whole thing with Ryan that has me so

spooked, Elizabeth realized. Unlike Jessica, Elizabeth didn't think that love was something you turned on and off like a switch. Jessica was always throwing herself into relationships, and things invariably ended the same way—with Jessica alone and looking for her next "true love."

That's not going to happen to me, Elizabeth reassured herself. *I'm not Jessica.*

She pulled a white dress off the rack and looked it over critically. *This could work,* she thought, shuffling through the others in search of her size. The dress was short and cut simply in a plain white fabric, but the full-length sleeves were a delicate, open lace.

"That one's really cute," a voice behind her back said. "Want to try it on?"

Elizabeth turned, startled, to face a young redheaded salesgirl.

"I have the same dress," the garrulous redhead volunteered. "I wore it to my boyfriend's house the other night, and, well . . ." She giggled, the color rising in her freckled cheeks. "Let's just say we had a *very* good time."

"Where's the dressing room?" Elizabeth asked immediately.

Elizabeth was thrilled when she saw her new reflection in the mirror. The dress was *perfect!* It had the simultaneous appearance of innocence and sex appeal that drove guys crazy. Not only that, the pure white lace looked outstanding with her tan showing through. Elizabeth's blue-green eyes sparkled with excitement as she smiled at her own reflection. Ryan was going to love this dress!

It wasn't until she had paid for her purchase and walked most of the way home that Elizabeth realized she was doing it again—she was acting like Jessica. What was she thinking about, buying a dress to interest Ryan when Tom was in Colorado, trusting her, waiting for her? *Well, Tom's not here and Ryan is,* Elizabeth rationalized.

Besides, hadn't Ryan made it clear that he was only interested in her friendship? Still . . . there was something in those guarded brown eyes. Something secret he tried not to show. Ryan might have thought he'd settled everything between them at the tower that afternoon, but Elizabeth thought that a moonlit walk on the beach was more likely to see things settled her way. Elizabeth honestly didn't know *what* she wanted from Ryan, but there was one thing she knew for sure: she didn't want to be his "friend."

The front door of the beach house was standing open as Elizabeth came up the walk.

"You did what?" Wendy squealed from the kitchen, laughing hysterically. "You're insane!"

Elizabeth could hear Winston laughing too and talking about hot dogs or something, but she didn't have time to stop and visit. Instead she hurried quickly up the stairs, hoping to beat Nina to the bathroom they shared. The pile of backpacks and sleeping bags in the dark corner by the staircase barely registered as Elizabeth rushed by. *Someone's friends must be crashing,* she thought.

Nina wasn't home yet, and Elizabeth rushed thankfully into the shower, hurrying to wash her long blond hair and apply a special conditioner. Then she wiped a clear circle in the steamy mirror and began putting on makeup, her wet hair wrapped in a turban of white towel. First she applied a smoky dark blue liner all the way around her eyes, then she followed it up with some eye shadow and two thick coats of mascara. Blush was unnecessary after so much sun, but Elizabeth spent a long time choosing just the right shade of lipstick. Finally she settled on a deep, rich mauve—not too pink, but definitely not red. *Very kissable,* she decided. Just right for the look she was going for with the white dress.

Elizabeth jumped as Nina banged loudly on the door. "What are you doing in there?" Nina demanded. "Writing a novel? Hurry up!"

Elizabeth's pulse quickened. "What time is it?" she called nervously through the closed bathroom door.

"It's after seven," Nina complained. "I've got to get ready too, you know."

"After seven!" Elizabeth exclaimed. Ryan was supposed to pick her up at seven thirty, and she still had to dry her hair and get dressed. All that makeup had obviously taken longer than she'd realized. "I'm coming!" she yelled, finishing her lipstick and opening the door.

Nina was standing in the hall barefoot in her lifeguard suit, still sandy from the beach. Her brown eyes widened noticeably when she saw Elizabeth.

"Wow!" she said, surprised. "What are you up to?"

"What do you mean?" Elizabeth asked, trying her best to sound innocent.

"I mean, what's with all the makeup?" Nina continued.

"Is it too much?" Panicked, Elizabeth turned to run back to the mirror.

"Not at all," Nina reassured her, stopping Elizabeth in her tracks. "You look great."

"Whew," Elizabeth breathed. "You scared me."

"You *ought* to be scared," Nina muttered as she stepped past her friend and into the bathroom, locking the door behind her.

"What's that supposed to mean?" Elizabeth demanded guiltily, shouting through the wall.

"I think you know," Nina answered, turning on the water and drowning out the possibility of continued conversation.

Am I that obvious? Elizabeth worried as she headed for her bedroom, hair dryer in hand.

Not that Nina was anyone to talk, of course. Elizabeth already knew all about Nina's date with Paul, just like Nina knew about Elizabeth's with Ryan. But while Nina had been honest about her confused feelings for Paul, Elizabeth had laid on the "Ryan-and-I-are-just-friends" routine with a trowel. Obviously she hadn't been that convincing.

Nina won't tell anyone, Elizabeth calmed herself as she sat in front of her dresser mirror and began drying her hair. The summer sun had lightened the blond tresses around her face to a shade near platinum, and the effect of her sun-streaked hair in conjunction with her deep golden tan and blue-green eyes was pretty spectacular. Add to that the fact that she was in the best physical condition of her life, and Elizabeth could draw only one conclusion—she'd never looked better.

She glanced nervously at the clock on the wall and saw that it was already seven twenty-five. Elizabeth had butterflies in her stomach as she quickly finished up her blow-drying and changed from her bathrobe into her new white dress— seven thirty exactly. She took one last, satisfied look in the mirror before she headed for the stairs.

She'd barely opened her bedroom door, however, when there was a huge ruckus in the living room. Elizabeth could hear loud voices and laughing, and Paloma was barking like he'd just apprehended an entire pack of burglars. Nina came charging out of her bedroom still wearing her bathrobe, and they both hurried downstairs to see what was happening.

"Isabella!" Nina exclaimed as she turned the corner just in front of Elizabeth.

"Danny!" Elizabeth said, coming up behind her friend. Ben and Jessica were there too, rounding out the rowdy group.

"I didn't know you guys were coming," Elizabeth added, pleased.

"Surprise!" Tom yelled, stepping out from behind the open front door, his arms extended toward her.

For a few seconds Elizabeth actually forgot to breathe. She was absolutely stunned. *What's Tom doing here?* she asked herself frantically, rooted to her spot by the stairs. She had barely formed that question, however, when another, truly awful thought occurred to her. Ryan would be here any minute! She had to *do* something—she had to get Tom out of the house before it was too late.

But it was already too late.

"Ryan!" Jessica exclaimed happily, spotting him through the open front door before Elizabeth could even move. "Come in and meet our friends."

Elizabeth felt as if she were trapped in a nightmare as Ryan walked into the living room and Jessica made the introductions. He looked amazing in a vintage Hawaiian shirt and shorts, a bouquet of daisies in his hand and a friendly smile on his handsome face.

"And this is Tom Watts," Elizabeth heard Jessica finish up. "Elizabeth's *boyfriend*."

The smile froze on Ryan's face as Tom bounded across the living room and scooped Elizabeth up in his arms, swinging her around full circle.

"Why are you just standing there?" Tom asked, smiling cluelessly. "Aren't you glad to see me?" Then, before she could answer, he added, "Wow, you're beautiful. I've missed you so much!"

"I've missed you too," she managed at last, her arms around Tom's neck and her eyes glued nervously on Ryan.

Jessica watched the scene in front of her with unadulterated pleasure. Her plan had worked even better than she'd dreamed!

After her friends had arrived, Jessica had taken them to the beach to look for Elizabeth, but her twin wasn't there. At Tower 2, Marcus told them Elizabeth had worked the Main Tower but was already off duty. They had gone looking for her in town after that, Jessica all the while kicking herself for missing the unexpected opportunity to spring Tom on Elizabeth right in front of Ryan. But obviously they hadn't found Elizabeth in town, either.

Now Jessica couldn't stop smiling as she watched her sister squirm uncomfortably in Tom's eager arms, her eyes fixed pleadingly on Ryan. This was *much* better than running into the lovebirds at the beach—Jessica had never dreamed she'd be lucky enough to catch them on an actual date!

"You look nice," Ryan said suddenly from beside her. "Are you ready to go?"

Jessica turned to see him extending the daisies in her direction, a polite smile on his lips. She couldn't resist a quick glance at Elizabeth, who was practically sagging with relief, before she took the bouquet triumphantly.

"Aren't you *sweet!*" Jessica exclaimed, playing her role as Ryan's date to the hilt. She held the flowers under her nose and inhaled with satisfaction. "*Where* did you say we're going for dinner again?"

"The Cove," Ryan answered quietly, naming one of the fanciest restaurants on the beach. Jessica positively glowed.

"Just give me five minutes," she told him, heading for the stairs to put on her new dress.

Tom and Elizabeth had moved to the center of the living room, where Tom was talking excitedly in a low, happy voice. *Poor Liz doesn't seem able to concentrate,* Jessica noted as she sailed by. She was so pleased with herself that she didn't see Ben at the base of the stairs until she'd practically tripped over him.

The look he gave her would have melted glass.

"So are we going to go to the rave or what?" Winston wanted to know.

"I said we would," Wendy answered, although she really didn't feel like it.

"Then don't you think we ought to get moving?" Winston asked impatiently. "It's almost nine. Everyone else has been gone for hours."

"For *an* hour," Wendy corrected him. "And they were all going to dinner first."

"Fools!" Winston clowned. "Why spend all that money at expensive restaurants when they could have dined at Chez Winnie's?"

He gestured grandly to the dirty cereal bowls and empty carton of milk on the kitchen table in front of them, and Wendy giggled.

"I can't imagine. Who would want to miss all this?"

The doorbell rang.

"Are you expecting someone?" she asked Winston.

He shook his head. "No. You?"

"No," she said, annoyed. "I hate it when people drop in—it's so rude. And why isn't Paloma barking?"

"I don't know." Winston followed her through the living room. "I just saw him a few minutes ago."

Wendy yanked the door open irritably, ready to give whoever was out there a piece of her mind.

"Pedro!" she exclaimed. "What are you doing here?"

"I came to take you to the rave," Pedro said, smiling hopefully as he produced an enormous bouquet of white roses from behind his back.

He was so handsome standing there in the lamplight that Wendy could have cried.

"I already told you that I'm going with my friends," she said stubbornly, keeping Pedro on the doorstep.

He looked past her into the living room. "With your *friend*, it looks like," Pedro observed. "Hi, Winston."

"Hey, Pedro," Winston responded, stepping up next to Wendy and forcing her to one side. "Come on in," he offered.

Wendy shot him a murderous look.

"What?" Winston protested.

"Thanks," Pedro said, walking into the living room. He was dressed all in black: black jeans, black T-shirt, and black cowboy boots. His long black hair was drawn back into a smooth ponytail, exposing a single gold hoop earring. The white roses he still held stood out sharply in contrast to his clothes. He'd never looked more irresistible, and Wendy felt herself starting to weaken.

"I'll go put those in water," she said suddenly, snatching the flowers from his hands, "but then Winston and I really have to go." She made her escape into the kitchen, her mind racing.

What is he trying to pull? Why doesn't he give up? A million questions closed in on her as she searched for something to use as a vase. The wine carafe Winston had selected the day before was still occupied, the bloodred flowers in gorgeous

142

full bloom on the counter where Wendy had left them. Desperate, Wendy grabbed a plastic orange juice pitcher from the cupboard and filled it at the sink. Roughly unwrapping the protective outer cellophane, she plunked Pedro's latest offering down into the clean, warm water. It was only then that she truly saw the flowers.

Wendy had never seen anything more perfectly white in her life than those snow white roses. And next to the deep, saturated red of the other bouquet, the new flowers were especially breathtaking.

Flesh and blood, Wendy mused. *Love and friendship. Desire and purity?* She was sure there was a message in there somewhere; she just wasn't sure what it was.

Oh, nuts. She gave up, becoming annoyed with herself. *They're just flowers. I'll go out there and get rid of Pedro, and then Winston and I will go to the rave and pretend to have fun.*

She pushed through the kitchen door with resolve, only to find Winston and Pedro chatting like two long-lost buddies.

"There you are, Wendy," Winston said happily. "Guess what? Pedro's coming with us. Isn't that great?"

Wendy put all the nastiness she could muster into the look she gave her so-called friend.

"What?" Winston protested again.

*　　　*　　　*

143

"I just wanted to spend some time alone with you before we joined the party," Tom said. "You're not upset, are you?"

"Of course not!" Elizabeth said, hoping her voice didn't sound as hollow to him as it did to her. "This is great."

They were walking together along the edge of the water, the moonlight brilliant overhead and the night still and warm. On any other night a romantic walk on the beach with Tom *would* have been great. But not on this night. Elizabeth felt so confused.

"Then come here," Tom said, taking her into his arms and kissing her deeply.

She held tightly to his tall, lean frame and kissed him back—trying to make things right, trying to forget about Ryan. But there was no fire in her kisses.

"Are you sure nothing's the matter?" Tom asked after a few minutes. "You seem . . . preoccupied."

"No! Nothing," she lied. "It's just that I didn't know you were coming. In fact, I can still barely believe you're here."

Tom laughed. "It was all Jessica's idea. I can't believe one of your sister's crazy schemes finally worked! That guy Ryan she's dating seems pretty nice—maybe he's having a good influence on her."

"*Jessica* invited you down?" Elizabeth asked, surprised.

"Yeah," Tom said. "Amazing, huh? She's usually too busy thinking about herself to worry about anyone else."

And this time is no exception, Elizabeth realized, silently furious. It all made sense now. She'd been sabotaged by her twin sister!

"Just a little farther," Paul assured Nina, leading her by the hand.

She followed reluctantly, looking back over her shoulder in the direction of the old cannery.

"But what are we doing out here on the pier?" she protested, pointing. "The rave is back there."

"What I want to show you is better than a rave," Paul answered. "I promise."

He dropped her hand and hurried on ahead. A few seconds later he turned and stepped off the edge of the pier, disappearing into the blackness below.

"Paul!" Nina screamed, expecting to hear a splash.

"What?" he answered, his voice only a few feet away.

Nina rushed to where Paul had gone over the edge and peered into the darkness. She saw now that he had stepped down onto some kind of small platform. A wooden ladder descended seaward from the edge of the platform, and Paul was already on it. "Come on," he urged. "This is going to be great."

"I'm not going anywhere until you tell me what we're doing," Nina insisted, standing stubbornly at the edge of the pier.

Paul laughed as he worked his way down toward the water below. "If you must know, Ms. Suspicious, my friend lent me his ski boat. I thought it would be fun to cruise around in the moonlight awhile before we go to the party."

"We'll *miss* the party," Nina worried.

"Are you kidding?" Paul asked, his voice floating up to her from farther and farther down the ladder. "That thing will be going for hours. Besides, I thought you said you liked fast boats."

"I do," Nina admitted, still hesitating on the edge of the pier.

Oh, what the heck, she thought, throwing caution aside. *A little ride in a ski boat never hurt anyone.*

She stepped onto the platform and began descending the ladder, glad she'd decided on the white shorts and flower-print top she was wearing instead of a dress. In a minute she was at the bottom and being helped into the tethered, rocking boat by Paul's strong hands.

"What did I tell you?" Paul demanded proudly. "Isn't she a beauty?"

Nina nodded her approval. It was a very hot boat, and Nina was suddenly excited to see what it could do. Together she and Paul cast off the lines and pushed away from the pier before he started the enormous outboard motor. The boat leapt underneath them with a roar, charging forward through the swells at a steadily increasing speed. In seconds they were planing, the front half of the boat completely out of the water as Nina and Paul tore dizzily along the shoreline, laughing and hooting with pleasure.

"Wow!" Nina screamed over the motor, "I'd love to take her skiing sometime."

"You think you're up to it?" Paul teased.

"I'm up to anything you're up to," she answered.

He smiled. "I was hoping you'd say that." He pushed the accelerator all the way to the limit.

The boat shot forward like a bullet, its hull just barely slapping the tops of the swells as it hurtled through the inky water at top speed. Landmarks on the shore went by in a blur as Paul held his course parallel to the beach. It was scary, but it was also incredibly exhilarating, and Nina held on tight, enjoying the cool salt spray in her face and the way the yellow beads in her hair clattered behind her in the wind.

She was really starting to get into it when the motor suddenly sputtered and died. The unexpected quiet assaulted Nina's ears as loudly as the high-powered engine had only a second before. The boat continued gliding forward through the water, gradually lost momentum, and finally stopped.

"What are you doing?" Nina asked, turning to Paul.

"Nothing," he answered, looking as surprised as she was. "It just died."

He turned the key in the ignition a few times, trying to restart the motor. The engine coughed, but nothing happened. "This is unbelievable!" Paul exclaimed angrily, slamming his hand down on the steering wheel.

"What's wrong with it?" Nina asked.

"I don't know," he answered. "The starter's working—it's like it's not getting any gas."

"Maybe the fuel lines are clogged," Nina suggested calmly, drawing on her long experience with boats.

"Maybe," Paul agreed, looking at her appreciatively. "But let's hope not. That'll be a major pain to fix out here—I don't even know if we have any tools."

The little boat tossed and drifted on the swells as Paul rummaged for a flashlight in the center console and pulled up the bilge hatches to begin checking the fuel lines. Nina meanwhile moved to the skipper's position in case Paul wanted her to try the engine again. She'd been standing at the wheel a few minutes, taking in the contrast between the calm night air and the sounds of Paul's earnest swearing, before it occurred to her to check the simplest thing of all.

They were out of gas.

"Good one, Paul," she said, her voice hard and cold. "How stupid do you think I am?"

"What?" he asked, standing up. He looked genuinely confused, but Nina wasn't going to be fooled by his innocent act again.

"You know darn well we're out of gas," she accused, pointing to the gauge.

"What?" Paul exclaimed, rushing to the console.

"Don't give me that." Nina practically spat. "I wasn't born yesterday, you know. This is the oldest trick in the book."

"What are you talking about?" Paul asked.

"Oh, please. It goes something like this—get girl in boat, run out of gas, have way with girl. Does that refresh your memory at all?"

"Nina! I swear I never had anything like that in mind," Paul pleaded. "My friend said I could use the boat, but he didn't tell me it needed gas."

"You've got two seconds to get the spare gas can from wherever you've hidden it," Nina told him icily, "or I'm out of here."

"Where are you going to go?" Paul asked soothingly, but with a hint of amusement in his voice too. "Just calm down." He reached to take her by the shoulders, but she shrugged him off furiously.

"Don't you dare touch me," she snapped, kicking off her tennis shoes. "I'm sick of you *and* your dirty tricks."

"What are you talking about? Nina! What are you doing?" Paul's panicky voice rose from behind her as she climbed up onto the gunwale. *"Nina!"*

But she'd already launched herself off the boat in a shallow, surface-skimming lifeguard dive. The cold, rough water was more of a shock than Nina had expected, but she quickly began a strong breaststroke, confident she'd make it to shore easily.

"Nina!" Paul yelled from behind her again. "That's too dangerous! Are you crazy? Everyone knows you should *always* stay with the boat."

"*You* stay with the boat," she fired back over her shoulder. "I never want to see you again."

The rave was even greater than Jessica had imagined. Sure, everyone had said it would be cool, but no one could have guessed she'd be going with Ryan. She adjusted a spaghetti strap on her red minidress and looked around the old abandoned warehouse with satisfaction.

The smell of dead fish had long since departed from the cannery's bare concrete floor and corrugated tin walls. In its place were the smells of a raging party in full swing: beer and sweat, perfume and cigarettes. The giant warehouse was strategically lit with colored lights and strobes that rhythmically illuminated the old pulleys and chains rusting in the steel rafters high overhead. A giant beer and juice bar was set up along the back wall, and a reggae band played on a raised round platform near the center of the room. The entire rest of the warehouse was essentially a dance floor, the only seating being the metal folding chairs that hugged the three remaining walls in a single tightly packed row.

"Isn't this fun?" Jessica leaned over to whisper in Ryan's ear. They were sitting by the door, next to Danny and Isabella. Jessica would rather have been dancing, of course, but she sure wasn't going to complain.

"Yeah," Ryan agreed noncommittally. Jessica followed his eyes to where Elizabeth danced with Tom. Those two lovebirds had come in late, but there were no visible signs of trouble in paradise. They hadn't stopped dancing once.

"Don't you think my sister and Tom make a great couple?" Jessica asked. "They're just so perfect for each other."

Ryan shrugged his agreement. It honestly looked to Jessica as if he didn't care one way or the other. This was going to be even easier than she'd thought! It was time to get serious.

Jessica put a hand on Ryan's leg and leaned up against him, pitching her voice so only he could hear. "You know, Ryan," she said. "I like to think I understand guys pretty well. I know, for instance, that you've been hurt."

The muscles of his thigh tensed beneath her fingers, and Jessica knew her guess was right on target.

"I've been hurt too," she continued. "You have

no idea how much. Elizabeth is . . . well . . . a little simpler. She's always had an easier road."

Ryan didn't say anything, but Jessica could tell he was listening.

"Tom is only her second serious boyfriend," Jessica went on. "And he's a great guy. It would be a shame to break them up."

"I have no intention of breaking them up," Ryan responded quietly.

Jessica smiled like the Cheshire cat.

"I'm glad to hear it," she whispered, her lips brushing against his ear. "Because my sister wouldn't have the faintest idea what to do with a guy like you even if she got him."

He turned to face her. "And you would, I suppose."

"You *know* I would," she assured him, leaning in closer, inviting him to kiss her.

His brown eyes bored intently into her blue-green ones, but Jessica held his gaze boldly, unflinchingly, challenging him to act. He reached for her, pulling her lips to within inches of his.

He's going to do it! Jessica thought excitedly, her entire body straining forward.

"*Ryan!* Jeez, I've been looking for you everywhere," Captain Feehan complained loudly from the floor right in front of their chairs. Ryan dropped Jessica instantly and sprang to his feet.

"What's up?" he asked.

Jessica seethed as she glared her displeasure at

Captain Feehan, but he didn't even look at her. Pulling Ryan a few paces away, he spoke quickly and urgently into his ear.

"No way!" Ryan said, with more emotion than Jessica had heard all night. "Let's go."

The two men turned and began walking rapidly toward the door.

"Ryan!" Jessica protested loudly, leaping up. "Where are you going?"

"Captain Feehan needs me," he answered simply. "Sorry." The two men slipped out the door and into the night.

"Can you believe that?" Jessica demanded indignantly of Isabella.

"Wow," Isabella agreed, shaking her head sympathetically.

"What was that all about?" Danny asked. "Why do the police want Ryan?"

"That's the stupidest part of all!" Jessica fumed. "A No Swimming sign blew down yesterday, and the whole town is acting like it's a federal crime or something."

Danny laughed heartily. "You can't seriously be telling me that the fabulous Jessica Wakefield just got dumped in favor of a No Swimming sign," he teased.

Jessica could barely hold her tongue as she turned her back on Danny and watched Elizabeth dance with Tom.

This isn't over, she vowed.

Chapter
Ten

Wendy stood on the porch, her heart pounding as Pedro fumbled for his key.

"Here it is," he said at last, holding it up and smiling awkwardly.

Wendy smiled back nervously. Never in her wildest dreams would she have imagined she'd end up at Pedro Paloma's house tonight.

"Whoa, Carlos!" Pedro yelled as he opened the door and something brown and furry made a break for the great outdoors. Pedro grabbed his dog by the collar just in time to keep him from disappearing into the night.

"You little devil," Pedro said, bending to look into the basset hound's big brown eyes. "Where do you think you're going?"

Carlos howled mournfully in reply, his mouth forming a perfectly round little *o*.

"Can't you see we have company?" Pedro

asked him. "It isn't gentlemanly to run out on a lady."

Carlos howled again, and Wendy laughed. The dog looked so ashamed of himself, it was almost comical.

Pedro stepped inside, pulling the low-slung dog behind him. "Come on in," he invited, smiling back at Wendy.

She walked into the entry, and Pedro closed the door behind her. "Can I take your sweater?" he offered.

Wendy blushed with embarrassment as she handed over her plain white sweater. The rest of her outfit consisted of faded jeans and a pinstriped button-down shirt. Not exactly romantic attire, let alone sexy. She'd dressed for a wild party in a rusty abandoned warehouse, not a dream date with Pedro Paloma.

"Would you like a drink?" Pedro asked.

"Just, umm . . . water would be fine," Wendy stammered. The unreality of the whole situation was starting to catch up with her.

"Make yourself at home." Pedro waved in the direction of the living room. "I'll be right back."

He left, presumably for the kitchen, Carlos on his heels.

Wendy stood fixed to her spot by the front door, taking in her surroundings. She could have killed Winston for inviting Pedro to tag along with them earlier that evening, but now everything was forgiven. Less than an hour after they'd arrived at the rave, Pedro had wheedled her out onto the dance floor. The next thing she knew, she was doing some kind of crazy Texas line dance and having the time of her life. From there things had progressed to slow dancing—*very* slow dancing. Wendy's cheeks flushed red as she remembered the tender, possessive way Pedro had looked at her as they danced, his lips so close to hers.

Pulling herself together, Wendy strode to the center of the large living room. The inside of Pedro's house was exactly as she'd imagined it would be. The sofa was soft black leather, and so were two nearby chairs. The furniture was arranged on one side of the room to make space for an enormous black piano at the other. Dark, built-in bookshelves and an entertainment center took up most of the wall across from the sofa, but bright white shutters and the whitewashed plaster walls in the rest of the room kept the dark furniture from overwhelming the space. The hardwood floor was whitewashed as well, and guitar cases of several shapes and sizes leaned in the corners.

"Plain water was too . . . plain," Pedro said, entering the room again. "I hope you like sparkling."

"Yes. Thanks," Wendy said shyly, taking the heavy crystal glass he offered and noticing that he'd put a curl of lemon peel in it too.

"Here's to second chances," Pedro proposed, holding out his own identical glass.

"Second chances," Wendy echoed weakly, her heart in her throat.

Their glasses clinked together, and Wendy sipped her water self-consciously. She was suddenly very glad that she hadn't asked for anything stronger. She couldn't help being frightened by the intensity of her feelings for Pedro.

Pedro walked to the stereo and put on a CD; then he lowered the lights. The quiet strains of classical Spanish guitar filled the room as he sat on the leather sofa, put his drink on the large glass coffee table, and motioned for Wendy to join him. She crossed the room awkwardly and sat on the couch, leaving room for at least two more people between them, but Pedro immediately scooted over, closing the gap. Carlos took the opportunity to make his move as well, curling up on the pastel rug at their feet. Wendy took in everything and sighed without intending to, without even realizing it. It was the single most romantic moment of her life.

"At the risk of spoiling the mood," Pedro said, "there's something I have to say to you. It's about our first date. . . ."

"Don't—" Wendy rushed to stop him. She didn't want to drag all those hurt feelings out into the light, not tonight, not right now.

But Pedro was insistent. "It's just that I, of all people, should know what it's like to be judged by appearances," he said sincerely. "I can't believe I was so insensitive."

"You!" Wendy exclaimed, stiffening. How could he possibly know what things were like for a plain girl like her? "If you're getting judged by *your* appearance, you must be doing awfully well, is all I can say," she added, not looking at him.

"But I'm *not*," he insisted. "Don't you see? I'm a good musician—I could be big. But no one wants to give me a serious chance. They look at me and say, 'He's just a pretty boy with a so-so voice,' and that's as far as I ever get. 'The Night' did all right as a single, but no one's offering me an album."

"Then they're stupid," Wendy said passionately, her gray eyes flashing. "Someday your name's going to be a household word."

"And there's something else I regret about our first date," Pedro said, taking both of her hands in his.

"What?" The fire that had given her courage a moment before was snuffing out just when she needed it most.

"I wish I'd made you realize that night how beautiful you are," he said.

Wendy pulled her hands from his roughly, her eyes filling with tears.

"Now you're just teasing me," she whispered hoarsely, turning her face away.

"No," Pedro insisted, putting a hand on her cheek and forcing her to look at him. "You're beautiful on the *inside*—your character, your convictions, they all come shining through. Tonight, when we were dancing, there wasn't a woman in the room who could hold a candle to you."

"You're serious?" Wendy whispered, awed.

"Totally." He bent his head toward hers. "*Te quiero,* Wendy," he breathed, just as their lips came together.

I love you too, she thought.

Wendy felt as if her feet were barely skimming the ground as she let herself soundlessly through the back door of the big Victorian house. It was very late, and she didn't want to wake the others. After all, tomorrow was the Fourth of July, and they were going to need all the strength they could get.

But not Wendy. She felt as if she could run on adrenaline for a week at least. Pedro's whispered declaration still rang in her ears—he loved her. Pedro Paloma loved *her.* She had to tell someone, but who? Then it occurred to her—her dog!

"Paloma!" she whispered loudly, planning to pour her heart out to her pet. But Paloma wasn't in the kitchen.

The dog wasn't in the living room either, although the twins' two guy friends from college were crashed out on the sofa and the floor. Wendy hurried quietly up the two flights of stairs to her attic bedroom, expecting to find Paloma sleeping on her bed, but her room was empty. Nervousness

159

began to nibble at the edges of Wendy's happiness. She ran up the two flights of stairs to check the attic.

"Jessica," Wendy called softly, knocking gently on her housemate's door, "is Paloma in there with you?"

"No!" Jessica returned grouchily, obviously unhappy to have been disturbed.

"Who is that?" Wendy heard another sleepy voice mumble.

"It's just Wendy, Izzy. Go back to sleep," Jessica whispered.

Wendy started down the stairs. She didn't want to worry, but she couldn't help it. She turned around. In another moment she was knocking on the door of Winston's ground-floor room.

"Winston!" she whispered urgently. "Are you awake?"

"I am now," he answered sleepily.

Wendy opened the door and practically charged in. Paloma wasn't with Winston either. Now she *was* panicked.

"I can't find Paloma!" she told her friend, forgetting to keep her voice down.

"He's not in the house?" Winston asked, sitting up and rubbing his eyes.

"I can't find him," Wendy repeated in a loud, worried voice.

They both heard the door to the adjacent bedroom open, and a second later Ben was standing in Winston's doorway, dressed only in rumpled red plaid boxer shorts.

"What's going on?" Ben demanded. "Paloma's missing?"

"I can't find him!" Wendy was near tears.

"That does it," Ben snapped. He stepped out of Winston's room and walked to the base of the stairs.

"*Jessica!*" he roared.

Even from two floors away, the volume of Ben's bellow almost gave Jessica a heart attack.

"What was that?" Isabella whispered, sitting up in her sleeping bag. Her pretty face was white with fear.

"I don't know," Jessica admitted, more than a little scared herself. "I mean, it's Ben, but I don't know what his problem is."

"Jessica!" Ben howled again.

"What's going on?" Jessica heard Nina demand loudly from the floor below. The whole house was probably awake.

"Maybe you'd better go see what he wants," Isabella suggested.

"Yeah," Jessica agreed reluctantly, getting out of bed and pulling on her bathrobe.

By the time Jessica got to the living room, the lights were on and everyone was there: Wendy, Winston, Nina, Elizabeth, Danny, Tom, and, of course, Ben, wearing nothing but boxers and an incredibly belligerent expression. Isabella was the only person who hadn't come running to see the show.

Jessica opened her mouth to ask what was going on, but before even a single word came out, Ben ripped into her.

"Where's Paloma?" he demanded. "You *lost* him, didn't you?"

"I lost him?" she returned, shocked. "Since when is he my responsibility? He's not even my dog!"

"I specifically asked you to watch him," Ben accused, his voice loud and angry.

And suddenly Jessica was angry too.

"Who died and made you king?" she fired back. "Who are *you* to tell me what to do?"

"Isn't that just like you?" he shouted in return. "You're so *selfish!* You don't even care that someone is trying to kill Wendy's dog—all you care about is making sure you don't take orders from anyone else."

At the mention of her dog's possible danger, Wendy burst into terrified tears. Her sobs mingled with the shouting as Winston lamely tried to comfort her.

"That's a lie!" Jessica exclaimed. "That dog was fine when Wendy got home. Am I supposed to watch him when his owner is here too?" she demanded caustically. "Maybe you could handcuff his leash to my wrist and I could watch him twenty-four hours a day!"

"That's the only way you'd have a prayer of succeeding!" Ben yelled, the disgust in his tone evident. "I can't believe they made you responsible for *people* when you can't even watch a *dog*. You know something? You're the most vain, shallow, self-involved person I've ever met!"

Ben's accusations echoed from the walls as Jessica faced her astonished friends and housemates. She had never been so humiliated—and over something so unfair! It was too much.

"I *hate* you!" she screamed at Ben, putting her entire heart into her words.

"What?" he said, clearly stunned.

But Jessica was too incensed to see that her blow had already landed.

"I've *always* hated you," she went on at top volume. "In fact, I hated you the very first second I saw you!"

There was a shocked, charged silence while everyone waited for Ben to respond.

"Funny," he grimaced at last, the pain in his blue eyes obvious. "That's when I started loving you."

Elizabeth watched as Ben strode purposefully to the door, pausing just long enough to grab his lifeguard jacket from the peg and throw it on over his boxers.

"Where are you going?" Jessica faltered behind him, her tone contrite.

"To find Paloma," Ben answered, his voice flat and dead. And then he was gone. The silence that descended on the room was disrupted only by Wendy's convulsive sobs.

"Come on, Wendy," Winston said, breaking the spell at last. "Let's get some flashlights and go look for Paloma too." He led his friend out in the direction of the kitchen, his arm around her heaving shoulders. They both stared daggers at Jessica as they walked by, Wendy's wet eyes still streaming.

"It's not my fault!" Jessica protested.

Suddenly Elizabeth felt cold, sad. She pictured Ben walking around alone in the dark and realized that she, as well as Jessica, had been selfish. She was so lucky to have Tom, yet she hadn't even appreciated him. Quickly she went to him, burying her face against his warm, bare chest as his arms closed protectively around her.

"I love you so much," she whispered hoarsely.

"I love you too," Tom reassured her quietly. "More than you know."

More than I deserve, that's for sure, Elizabeth thought, choking back tears of remorse. It had taken the fight between Jessica and Ben to remind her how much Tom meant to her.

Meanwhile Danny, looking greatly embarrassed by the entire incident, had climbed back into his olive-drab sleeping bag. "Uh, how about lights-out?" he suggested.

"Good idea," Nina agreed, walking over to switch off the living-room lamp. "Are you coming, Elizabeth?"

Elizabeth lifted her head from Tom's broad chest and nodded tearfully. She'd been wrong to pursue Ryan. So wrong. Tomorrow she'd make it up to Tom—for everything.

"I needed this tonight like I needed a hole in the head," Nina told Jessica angrily as the three girls climbed the stairs together. "I had a horrible date tonight, and tomorrow is the biggest work-day of the summer—you could at least have let us sleep."

"But I didn't *do* anything!" Jessica insisted. "It was Ben!"

"You know what, Jessica?" Nina said as they reached the second-floor landing. "I don't want to hear it." She went into her bedroom and slammed the door behind her.

Jessica winced. No one understood how horrible she felt. Even *she* didn't understand it. How could she have said such awful things to Ben? And then for him to say he *loved* her after that. . . .

"Liz!" Jessica appealed, turning toward her twin.

"Don't come whining to me," Elizabeth whispered. Her voice was very low, but there was no mistaking her cold, angry tone. "And don't think I don't know why you invited Tom down here, either."

"I thought you'd be glad . . . ," Jessica began, but Elizabeth cut her off.

"You thought nothing of the sort!" she whispered, furious. "I don't appreciate being ambushed, Jess."

"I swear it wasn't like that!" Jessica lied desperately, trying to convince herself as much as her sister.

"Oh, go to bed," Elizabeth said, disgusted. "You've done enough damage for one day, and I think you've run out of people to hurt." She closed her bedroom door right in Jessica's face.

You've hurt enough people for one day, Jessica repeated to herself as she climbed the second flight of stairs to her own room. Immediately Ben's stricken expression appeared before her. She hadn't even meant those things she'd yelled at him.

Isabella was wide awake, of course, when Jessica opened the door. "What was that about?" she asked, her gray eyes enormous. "What I could hear sounded brutal."

"You're lucky you stayed up here," Jessica told her, flipping off the light and climbing back into bed.

"But what was Ben so mad about?" Isabella wanted to know.

"Nothing," Jessica said. "Wendy's stupid dog."

But Jessica knew it wasn't really Paloma that had Ben so worked up. It was what she'd done to Elizabeth and Tom. It was the way she kept

166

throwing herself at Ryan. It was . . . everything. She could never face him again. She knew what she had to do.

"I want to go home with you when you leave tomorrow," Jessica told Isabella suddenly.

"What?" Isabella said. "Why?"

"I hate it here!" Jessica exclaimed passionately. "Everyone's so unfair, and lifeguarding's such a pain. I want to go home with you—for good."

"Okay," Isabella said slowly. "If that's what you want."

"It is," Jessica assured her. She'd had all she could take of Sweet Valley Shore.

Chapter
Eleven

Where is he? Nina worried. She looked down from the Main Tower at the huge, colorful crowd streaming onto the sand and her hands gripped the railing hard. It was nine in the morning on the Fourth of July and Ryan hadn't shown up for work.

It would be just like him to desert us when we need him most, Nina thought, provoked, but then quickly reversed herself. *No,* she argued mentally, *he's been fine this year. Something must really be wrong.*

It had been a shock to the entire Sweet Valley Shore Squad to find that Ryan wasn't at his post when they'd arrived at the beach. Ryan was *never* late to work—after all, he lived there. But it had been an uglier shock to the returning lifeguards—the ones who remembered last summer—than to the rookies. Wendy and Nina had immediately exchanged worried glances. They'd waited for

Ryan until nine fifteen, then Nina had made her decision.

"I think we'd better get started," she'd announced, forcing as much false confidence into her voice as she could. "Ryan will probably be here any second, but since I'm second-in-command, I'm going to go ahead and make the tower assignments. Elizabeth, you're with me. Ben and Kerry, Tower 2. Wendy and Paula, Tower 3. Marcus and Jessica, South Tower. Let's hit it, people!"

To Nina's immense relief, everyone had taken their assignments without grumbling and gone off to do their jobs. Even Jessica, who had come to Nina's room earlier that morning and announced that she was quitting—effective immediately.

"I can't work with the people on our squad another minute," Jessica had said, tossing her blond hair for emphasis. "I quit." She'd stood framed in Nina's doorway, declining to step inside.

"Why?" Nina had gasped.

But Jessica had just folded her arms stubbornly across the front of her burgundy bathrobe and refused to answer. After the blowout between Jessica and Ben the night before, Nina wasn't surprised that Jessica wanted to flee the scene of the crime, but she still couldn't afford to lose a guard on the Fourth—even one as on-again, off-again as Jessica.

"Look, Jess," Nina had practically begged. "You're just upset right now. You can't let us down on the Fourth of July! We need you."

"Sorry," Jessica had said, heading down the hall.

"Just for today!" Nina had called after her. "Please!"

There had been more pleading, bargaining, and even some bickering, but finally Jessica had sulkily agreed to work one more day. There *was* a condition, though: she'd do it only if she didn't have to work with Ben.

"I won't talk to him. I won't work with him. I won't have anything to do with him," Jessica had said, her voice tight. "Try to make me, and I'll walk out. I swear I will."

Nina had agreed, pretending it was a major concession, but she'd never have risked putting the two of them together anyway. When they'd reported in for duty, they refused to even look at each other.

Everything was unraveling. Nina knew that Elizabeth wanted the day off too, to spend with Tom. She was planning to ask Ryan for it the second he showed up, still happy in the supposition that he *would* be showing up.

It was the most important day of the entire beach season, and the squad was falling apart. And that was all *before* Ryan had bailed. Nina's hands hurt from gripping the railing so hard. *Please give me the strength to hold this squad together,* she prayed. *Please don't let anyone get hurt out here today.*

170

The telephone in the glassed-in portion of the tower shrilled, making Nina jump. "I'll get it," she told Elizabeth. "You're on watch."

Elizabeth nodded coolly as Nina ran inside. Just one more thing to worry about—it was pretty obvious that Elizabeth had an attitude about Nina's comment regarding the date-that-hadn't-happened with Ryan the night before. At this point Nina honestly didn't care if Elizabeth talked to her or not—just as long as she took orders.

"Main Tower!" Nina barked, reaching the phone and snatching it off the hook.

"Hi, Nina," Ryan's voice said on the other end.

"Ryan! Thank goodness!" Nina exclaimed. "Where *are* you?"

"I'm a little tied up. You're going to have to take over today."

"But . . ."

"I'll be there later if I can," he said. "I have to go now."

"Ryan!" Nina protested, but the phone was already dead in her hand.

Nina groaned aloud as she replaced the receiver. The Fourth of July was starting out with more of a whimper than a bang.

"That was Ryan," Nina said, walking back out to the railing. "He's not going to be here until later on."

171

Elizabeth nodded acknowledgment. Her face was expressionless, but inside was total turmoil. *Great,* was her first thought, *now I'm probably going to have to work the whole day.* She'd told Tom she'd do her best to get the day off, and she'd really intended to give the attempt her all. She owed him that much to make up for her past mistakes.

"Did Ryan say when he's coming in?" Elizabeth asked Nina, breaking her silence at last. It still made her mad the way Nina had jumped to conclusions about her nonexistent relationship with Ryan, but she couldn't ice her all day.

"No." Nina shook her head. "We'll just have to do the best we can without him until he gets here."

For the first time Elizabeth noticed the stress in Nina's voice and saw the worry etched on her friend's anxious face.

"What's the matter?" Elizabeth asked, concerned.

"It's just a big day, you know?" answered Nina. "The biggest, actually. His timing couldn't be worse."

"He'll be here soon," Elizabeth soothed, sure she was right.

"Yeah," Nina said.

But Elizabeth could tell that for some reason Nina didn't believe it.

Jessica climbed the stairs of the South Tower, her rescue buoy clutched in one wet hand and her long hair dripping.

"False alarm, huh?" commiserated her tower partner, Marcus.

"I hate it when kids do that," Jessica griped.

"They only seem to do it when they know it's *your* turn," Marcus teased, letting his eyes roam significantly over her wet bathing suit. "None of those little boys ever want *me* to come out and get them."

Jessica smiled in spite of herself.

"Yeah," she agreed. "I thought I'd noticed a pattern."

"I'd have done the same thing when I was thirteen," Marcus told her. "Who *wouldn't* want to be rescued by a total babe like you? That kid'll probably live off this for the rest of the year."

"Thanks," said Jessica, her smile broadening a little. At least someone appreciated her.

She still couldn't believe the way the whole house had turned on her the night before. Okay, so maybe Elizabeth was a tiny bit justified, but Nina? And Wendy and Winston were totally out of line—it wasn't Jessica's fault that Wendy's dog was missing. And *Ben!* Jessica's throat closed up as the tears tried to force their way past her lashes. She couldn't even think about Ben.

Isabella is my only true friend, Jessica told herself, *the only real friend I have.*

But even Isabella had refused to sneak out of Sweet Valley Shore at dawn like Jessica had wanted her to.

"The guys have to be considered too," Isabella had insisted. "And they're looking forward to a day at the beach. We'll all go tonight after the fireworks, like we planned."

So Jessica had had to wake Nina up and tell her she was quitting, but *that* hadn't worked either—here she was in the South Tower despite all her efforts to the contrary. It was as if it was her destiny or something.

"Those guys with the radio are getting out of hand," Marcus announced. "I'm going to go caution them."

"Right," Jessica said, snapping back to the present and assuming a watch position at the railing.

Just let me get through this day, she thought as she watched Marcus cross the sand toward an extremely rowdy group of fraternity brothers. The beach was getting wilder by the second, and it wasn't even noon.

No—cancel that, Jessica amended, looking guiltily up the beach toward Tower 2. *Just let me get through this day without having to talk to Ben!*

"What are you doing here, Wendy?" Nina demanded, her tone unreasonably harsh. "Why aren't you on your tower?"

Elizabeth looked over from her position at the rail in time to see Wendy gain the tower deck. After the way Nina had just snapped at her,

Elizabeth expected Wendy to be mad, but the only emotion Elizabeth saw on Wendy's face was genuine concern.

"Lunch break," Wendy explained evenly. "Paula's covering. Hear anything else from Ryan?"

"No," Nina said, the worry in her brown eyes obvious. "Not since the first time."

Wendy shook her head. "I really hope he's okay," she said fervently.

"Me too," Nina said.

"Of course he's okay," Elizabeth butted in nervously. All the significant glances and cloak-and-dagger stuff were finally starting to get to her. "I mean, why wouldn't he be?" she demanded.

But Nina and Wendy just looked at her, identical vacant stares on their faces.

"What!" Elizabeth insisted. "If it affects the squad, I have a right to know."

"It's just that . . . well . . . we're afraid he might have disappeared again," Wendy finally admitted.

"Disappeared!" Elizabeth cried. "What are you talking about?"

"I've got to get back to my tower," Wendy announced uneasily, making a getaway down the stairs. "I'll check back with you later, Nina," she called up from the sand before she bolted down the beach.

"Nina!" Elizabeth exclaimed, turning to her best friend. "What's going on?"

Nina faced Elizabeth with obvious reluctance. "I don't know how much I should tell you," she said at last.

"How about all of it?" Elizabeth suggested, her apprehension growing by the second.

"It's just that last summer . . . well . . . Ryan wasn't always the perfect lifeguard," Nina faltered. "I know that all *you've* seen so far is this totally together, totally committed guy—but there's another Ryan, too."

"What do you mean?" Elizabeth demanded.

Nina shrugged. "Last summer there were a few times Ryan didn't show up for work. Sometimes for days. We wouldn't know where he was or what was going on. And then he'd just come back. No explanations. Ever."

"I don't believe it!" Elizabeth gasped. How could Ryan run out on them? And today of all days? He'd always seemed so dedicated—could Elizabeth have completely misread him?

And then another thought occurred to her—why hadn't Nina told her this before?

"Why didn't you tell me about this earlier?" Elizabeth asked. "You know Ryan's my friend."

"He's my friend too," Nina reminded her, an edge to her voice. "And what good would telling you before have done? Everyone deserves a second chance."

"But this is serious, Nina!" Elizabeth insisted.

"Yes, it is," Nina agreed. "But try not to judge

Ryan too harshly. The pressures of his job . . . well, you have no idea. Sometimes I guess it's too much for him."

"I think I know about the pressures of the job," Elizabeth returned sharply, not liking the way Nina was talking down to her.

"Really?" Nina countered. "Why don't you tell me that again after a child drowns on *your* shift?"

Elizabeth had known that a child had died the summer before, but she'd never imagined Ryan was the lifeguard in charge when it happened. "Poor Ryan," she whispered, all the fight knocked out of her. She couldn't even conceive of how awful that would be.

"It wasn't his fault," Nina defended him quickly. "But he blames himself anyway."

"Because he was in charge," Elizabeth guessed.

"Yeah," Nina said uneasily, looking out to sea. "Something like that."

"I can't believe it," murmured Elizabeth. If only she could see him! She needed to know where he was, to know if he was all right. Then something else occurred to her. "But why *today*?" she asked Nina suddenly. "Why would he desert us *today*?"

"The only thing I can figure is that seeing you with Tom last night pushed him right back over the edge," Nina answered bluntly.

"That's not fair!" Elizabeth replied hotly. "Ryan and I are just friends. He's *always* known I have a boyfriend."

"Uh-huh," Nina said, her eyes on the surf. The sarcastic way she said it made Elizabeth furious.

"Look who's talking!" Elizabeth shot back angrily. "What about Paul?"

Nina's dark face clouded dangerously. "What about him?" she challenged.

Chapter
Twelve

Wendy ran halfway back to her tower before she slowed to catch her breath. There was no way she'd wanted to be there when Nina broke the news about Ryan to Elizabeth. She wasn't blind—she knew Elizabeth was going to feel betrayed. But Wendy felt betrayed too, and she had problems of her own. Paloma was still missing, and she was worried sick.

The only thing keeping her going was Pedro. *Te quiero, Wendy,* she heard him say over and over in her head. Wendy knew that literally translated the words meant "I want you," but she'd paid attention in Spanish class. In English *te quiero* would be more like "I love you." Not that there was anything wrong with "I want you," either. A happy smile spread across Wendy's face, lighting her perfect complexion. There was only one place to go after *te quiero: te amo,* the expression of romantic love saved for that one special person.

Taking a wrinkled picture of Paloma from her shorts' pocket, Wendy scanned the beach. She knew that if she wanted to find her dog, she was going to have to do something about it. She spotted a group of young teenage guys just ahead and, putting her shyness aside, approached them resolutely.

"Hi," she said loudly, stopping a few feet away.

"Uh, hi," the cutest one said, leaping up and vainly trying to brush the sand off his wet bathing suit. "How's it going?"

"Okay," Wendy answered shortly, holding out her photograph. "I'm looking for this dog. Have any of you seen him?"

The boys took the picture and passed it around. "No," each one said reluctantly in turn.

"We'll help you look, though!" a guy with dreadlocks offered. "Hang out with you all day if you want."

His buddies had already finished their snickering and elbowing before Wendy realized what was going on. They were *flirting* with her!

"Uh, thanks," she declined, laughing in disbelief, "but the tower has a weight limit."

"Beautiful *and* funny," the cute one said, leering at her appreciatively. "Just the way I like 'em."

Wendy was in shock as she continued down the beach. Nothing like that had happened to her before—ever. She held her head higher, prouder as she walked. A month in the sun had turned her long, once mousy hair more golden than brown, and the rigorous daily exercise had left its mark on her body, too. But no one had noticed before today.

No one had noticed until Pedro noticed.

"Hey, gorgeous!" someone yelled. Wendy turned her head to see that she was being addressed by an extremely handsome guy in his twenties. She waved hesitantly and continued on her way, her cheeks flaming. A series of wild catcalls sounded from behind her as her admirer's friends joined in.

It's just like Cinderella, Wendy realized, awed. Except that *her* prince wore black cowboy boots.

"Oooooh, Daddy! Daddy, yuck!" a hysterical five-year-old girl screamed just inches from Jessica's ear.

Jessica winced with annoyance as she dipped the old guy's foot back into the already gory bucket of fresh water. Every time she'd get the cut cleaned out, it would be running blood again before she could bandage it. It looked pretty bad, and Jessica wasn't sure exactly what to do.

I knew all that glass patrol was a waste of time! she thought irritably as she probed with her tweezers for any remaining fragments of the broken beer bottle her patient had stepped on.

"I want Mommy!" a little boy in sandy diapers wailed from her other side, clearly terrified.

Of course the six kids the guy had with him weren't making her job any easier.

"Everybody just calm down," Jessica snapped, more harshly than she had intended. All six children immediately started crying.

Jessica almost felt like crying herself. All she'd wanted was to get out of town and out of life-guarding.

"I'm sorry," she apologized to the children's father, trying to stop the bleeding by applying pressure with a clean white towel. "I didn't mean it to come out like that."

"It's okay," he said kindly. "I understand."

Jessica pressed down harder with the towel, hoping it would work this time.

When the guy had limped up to the tower, his hands covered in blood from trying to dig out the glass with his fingers, Marcus had chickened out immediately.

"*You* help him," he'd begged Jessica.

"Why me?" Jessica had protested. "It's your turn."

"I know, but the sight of that much blood makes me sick," Marcus had confessed in an urgent whisper, looking down the tower and shuddering. "*Please*, Jessica! I'll get the next *three*."

Jessica had to admit she was starting to feel a little nauseous herself as she lifted the blood-soaked towel and examined the raw white flesh inside the deep, open gash. There was no way she was going to fix this one with a Band-Aid.

"I think you're going to need some stitches," she said reluctantly, expecting her patient to argue.

"I'm sure of it." He smiled, perfectly calm. "If you can just get it bandaged up long enough for me to drive to the hospital, I'd really appreciate it."

"You can't drive like this," Jessica protested. "Marcus!" she yelled up the tower. "Call for the Jeep."

Marcus flashed her a grateful thumbs-up and went into the tower to radio.

"I'm just going to try to keep this from bleeding too much until you get to the doctor," Jessica said, piling heaps of gauze against the man's wound and winding white adhesive tape tightly around the foot and dressing. Unbelievably blood immediately started showing through, and Jessica pulled the tape even tighter. She could hear the Jeep approaching now as, relieved, she wrapped the man's bandaged foot in another clean towel and taped that on too. If they could get him to the hospital, a doctor would stitch him up and everything would be fine.

The Jeep turned around behind her, and Jessica heard the driver get out and open the passenger's door.

"Your daddy's going to see a nice doctor," Jessica told the crying children gently, hoping to calm them down. "And *you* all get to ride in a real lifeguard's Jeep—with a big light on top!"

"Cool!" the oldest boy exclaimed. He looked about eight. His sobs immediately deteriorated into sniffles as he stared wide-eyed over Jessica's shoulder at the Jeep. Thankfully the others followed his example.

"Let me help you in, sir," a familiar deep voice offered politely at Jessica's back.

Jessica stiffened with a mixture of anger and embarrassment. She'd been so busy with her patient that she'd never thought to look who was driving the Jeep. But now she couldn't believe her ears—Nina had sent Ben!

"Thank you, son," the man accepted gratefully as Ben pulled him to a one-footed standing position and supported him on his strong shoulders.

"You kids all pile in the back now," Jessica ordered, helping them climb in while studiously avoiding looking at Ben. She heard the passenger door shut and then, finally, the driver's door too.

Just get out of here! she thought, willing Ben away.

The Jeep turned around and headed south toward the hospital. Then, for some inexplicable reason, it turned and reapproached the tower. Jessica backed quickly toward the stairs, but the Jeep drove directly to her.

"I just wanted to say thank you," Jessica's former patient shouted in explanation, leaning out the window to address her more closely.

"It was nothing," Jessica said, embarrassed.

She looked down at the pile of bloody towels, hoping to avoid Ben's eyes. The water in the first-aid bucket looked like barely diluted blood, and for the first time Jessica noticed that there was blood all over the sand, too, and on her own hands and feet.

"It was a *lot*," the man insisted. "Thank you."

"You're welcome," she told him, looking up reluctantly.

The father smiled, satisfied, and settled back into his seat. Jessica immediately tried to avert her eyes again, but she wasn't quick enough—they locked with Ben's. Ben's intense gaze held hers, and what Jessica saw there literally took her breath away. It was the very last thing she'd expected.

It was respect.

"So what's *this* thing, then?" Tom asked, lifting something off the counter inside the tower and shouting through the glass.

In spite of all her good intentions to make things up to him, Elizabeth had to count to ten before she answered.

"I already told you I can't be turning around every five seconds to answer questions," she shouted from her position at the railing. "If you want to show me something, bring it out here."

A moment later he was at her side. "So?" he asked, holding out the object of his fascination.

"It's a whistle," she told him, unable to believe

he'd waste her time with such a stupid question.

"But I'll bet it's some special *kind* of whistle," Tom pressed.

"Yeah," Elizabeth snapped. "A loud one. On a string."

Tom had only been at the tower an hour and he was already driving her crazy. He wasn't supposed to be there at all—if Ryan had shown up, he'd never have allowed it—but Nina was letting it slide as a favor to Tom. Elizabeth wished she wasn't. Now Nina was on a break, and Elizabeth and Tom were about to have a fight.

But to Elizabeth's surprise, Tom just laughed. "Gee, I'm not getting on your nerves, am I?" he asked, in a way that made it clear he already knew the answer.

"I'm sorry, Tom," she apologized, taking her eyes off the waves for just a second. "It's just that I'm so stressed out. This is the *Main Tower* on the busiest day of the year. Do you have any idea how much responsibility that is?"

"Yeah," he said. "I think I'm starting to. I probably shouldn't even be here, right?"

"Right," she agreed, relieved he understood. "Maybe you could hang out with Danny and Isabella for a little while?"

"I came down here because I wanted to be with *you*," Tom reminded her.

"I know, and I'm sorry," she said. "But we can be together tonight, okay? We'll have some dinner, watch the fireworks. . . . It'll be fun."

186

"Okay," Tom agreed good-naturedly. "And anyway, there is something I kind of wanted to do." He checked his watch. "It's only three o'clock. If I leave now, I can still make it to the boardwalk in time for the Battle of the Buns."

"The *what?*" Elizabeth laughed.

"Didn't Winston tell you? He's fighting a giant hot dog."

"Winston in a fight?" Elizabeth said, alarmed. "No, he didn't tell me."

"Well, calm down," Tom said, "because the whole thing's rigged. From what I can gather, it's going to be more like professional wrestling than an actual fight. It's just a big show for the tourists."

Elizabeth shook her head, smiling. "Only Winston . . ."

"Hey, Wendy, isn't that your dog?" Paula asked, lowering her binoculars.

"Where?" Wendy asked excitedly, straining forward against the railing.

Paula pointed toward the water a short distance up the beach. "He's coming this way."

It *was* Paloma! The big mutt was racing south along the water's edge as if he'd just been shot out of a cannon. His long, shaggy hair was soaked and sandy, but he was obviously having the time of his life.

"Oh, thank goodness," Wendy breathed, tears of relief pricking her eyes. Dogs weren't allowed on the beach, but if she could catch him, she could hide him in the tower until quitting time.

"Go get him," Paula offered, reading her mind. "I'll cover the tower."

"Thanks," Wendy said gratefully, running down the stairs.

Paloma was already almost even with the tower, and Wendy couldn't remember ever having seen him run so fast. He was practically flying down the sand at the edge of the water, scattering castles, toys, and toddlers in his wake, but to Wendy it was the most beautiful sight she'd ever seen. The big dog radiated pure, unspoiled joy.

"Paloma!" Wendy called, running forward to greet him.

But he couldn't hear her voice over the surf and the screaming crowd. In another instant he'd passed the tower, still careening south at top speed.

"Go after him," Paula yelled. "I'm okay."

Wendy nodded and took off running. It was only a matter of seconds, though, before she realized it was hopeless. There was no way she was going to catch him unless he slowed down or, even better, stopped. "Paloma!" she screamed at his back, but his speed didn't falter. Wendy stood helplessly at the edge of the water, watching her pet disappear like a comet. Then, suddenly, Wendy caught sight of something else far away down the beach—a big white van.

"Oh no," she groaned out loud. There were only three groups that routinely drove on the beach: the lifeguards, the sheriff's department, and animal control. Of those only animal control had vans. If they managed to pick Paloma up, it would mean a hefty fine for her.

"Keep running, Paloma," Wendy encouraged under her breath as the animal control officer got out of the van and strolled in the direction of the water. "Just keep running."

But Paloma didn't listen. He was almost even with the officer when the man extended his hand in the dog's direction. Paloma put on the brakes like a cartoon dog, throwing up a rooster tail of water as he skidded to a stop in front of the officer and snagged the dog-biscuit bribe. The officer patted Paloma on the head, took him by the collar, and led him off toward the van, Paloma's tail wagging like crazy the entire time.

"Well, at least he's safe," Wendy comforted herself as she walked dejectedly back to her tower.

"Step up! Gather around, people!" Winston crowed in his best circus barker imitation. The steaming boardwalk was packed beyond Winston's wildest, most imaginative dreams. People of all descriptions jostled and pushed to get a better view, and the smells of sweat, beer, and suntan oil were almost overwhelming.

"See Hot Dog Howie dominate the Weenie

Boy in the burger suit," Howie yelled from the other side of the "ring" he and Winston were clearing. "See those tender round buns hit the boardwalk so hard they split."

"See Hot Dog Howie awaken into reality when he meets the *true* Bun King of the Boardwalk," Winston countered at the top of his lungs. "*We'll* see who the real weenie is."

He could practically smell the money.

"Ten bucks on the hamburger," Tom Watts shouted, right on cue. Winston tried to keep the smile from his face as his friend launched the betting with the money Winston himself had given him.

"Sucker!" Howie taunted.

"I'll take that action," a mean-looking guy in puke green Bermuda shorts offered, elbowing through the crowd toward Tom.

"I'll put five on the hot dog," Nina called hesitantly. Winston had caught her walking by on her break and had immediately coerced her participation too. A teenage boy quickly covered Nina's bet.

The beauty of the thing was that it didn't matter if Winston won or lost—that wasn't how they were going to make their money.

"Twenty on the hot dog," a woman's voice offered loudly. Within minutes the betting had reached and exceeded the frenzy of the day before, with fifty and even one-hundred-dollar bets being called out and answered all over the place.

As soon as the action slowed down Winston held up one hand for silence. With the crowd watching intently, he took a red plastic beach pail and placed it near the edge of the ring.

"Obviously my *colleague*," he sneered the word, "and I have no problem with you people making a little money on our grudge match. But remember, this is a serious rivalry—there's a lot at stake—"

"What the *weenie* here is trying to say," Howie interrupted rudely, strutting his stuff around the ring, "is that he's afraid he'll be out of a job once I kick his puny butt. So if all you people who win big on me drop, say, ten or twenty percent of your take into the weenie's bucket, he won't go hungry next month."

There was a flurry of betting on Howie.

"*Au contraire,* Hot Dog Hair," Winston countered, causing the crowd to scream with delighted laughter—Howie had shaved his head for the big event. "I'm far more concerned about you catching cold. The proceeds of this match will buy my poor, deluded opponent a stocking cap," Winston announced to the onlookers.

"That's it," Howie roared, launching himself at Winston.

It was a beauty of a fight. Winston and Howie had met early and in secret to choreograph their moves, Winston wanting the Battle of the Buns on the Boardwalk to be remembered for generations. There were choke holds and bun grabs and even pirouettes. There was pushing and shoving and some truly inspired name-calling. And, more than that, there was literally a cast of hundreds—the ranting, wagering crowd.

"Getting tired, Burger Boy?" Howie taunted as he and Winston whirled each other around and around in a move that could have come straight from the Ice Capades.

That was their signal.

"You wish," Winston grunted loudly in return. He let go of Howie and the two of them careened backward into the crowd. Winston was entirely satisfied that they'd already given the people the show they'd come to see. From here on out he and Howie would just try to trip each other until one of them actually fell. No one was taking a dive, though—it wouldn't be fair to the bettors. Winston crouched low and moved in on the hot dog.

"Here he comes!" someone screamed, sensing the change in pace. "The hamburger's serious now!"

"Howie! Howie!" a couple of drunks standing on a nearby bench chanted.

Winston and Howie circled each other slowly, cautiously, looking for an opportunity. Winston made a lunge and Howie stepped back quickly, deftly grabbing Winston's tomato slice in the process. Winston whirled to free himself, but immediately realized his error. His back was to Howie now and he couldn't get away.

Howie didn't make him suffer long. In one swift stroke he pushed the backs of Winston's knees forward, causing Winston's legs to buckle and drop him, stomach bun first, to the boards. It was painless and fast, and the crowd went crazy.

There were cheers and jeers all over the place as people collected on their bets. Winston rolled over and sat stunned on his oversize back bun as Howie waved his clasped fists above his head in triumph. Then he went to retrieve the red plastic bucket.

"Ante up, people," Howie shouted, strutting through the crowd with the outstretched bucket. "Time to pay your dues!"

"Are you okay, Winston?" Nina asked in a worried voice, coming to crouch at his side. Tom Watts knelt on the boards beside her.

"Of course," he assured them. "I just had no idea Howie could move so fast, that's all."

Howie grinned as he walked by them with the rapidly filling bucket. "He acts like I haven't been doing this every season for the last ten years," he remarked, just loud enough for Winston and his friends to hear.

"A ringer!" Tom exclaimed, exploding with laughter. "Winston, you've been taken!"

Winston shook his brown curls sadly, still sitting on his bun. "And I thought this was my idea. When will I learn that *all* of these guys are smarter than me?" he groaned, remembering how Harry had hoodwinked him too.

"Ah, cheer up, kid." Howie walked over with a brimming bucket. "We made a bundle, and we'll split it even-steven, just like we said."

Winston *did* feel better when he saw the packed plastic bucket spilling over with fives and tens. "Wow!" he said. "How much is that?"

"A lot. Come over to my cart and we'll count it." Howie reached out a hand and pulled Winston back onto his feet.

They'd just finished counting the bills and Winston was pocketing his half happily, secure in the knowledge that the money he'd made that afternoon would get him through the month, when a terrified scream split the afternoon. Someone was in trouble on the beach.

Nina reacted immediately, leaping over the boardwalk rail and taking off across the sand at a dead run. With only a second's hesitation Winston and Tom followed.

"My friends! My friends!" a college-age girl in a pink bikini was screaming hysterically as Winston pulled up even with Nina. "Their boat . . . they can't swim!"

"Pay attention!" Nina ordered, gripping the girl by the arms. "How many friends?"

"Six," the girl said, slipping out of Nina's hands and sinking to the sand. "Oh, please," she sobbed, completely out of control. "They're all drunk, too."

Winston squinted against the glare as he tried frantically to make out six victims in the water, but the only thing he saw was an inflatable toy boat, much too small to carry six adults, bobbing upside down on the waves. The girl in the bikini saw it too and started vomiting.

Winston crouched beside her in his hamburger suit and tried to pat her back reassuringly. "Don't worry," he whispered past the lump in his throat.

He'd never felt so helpless in his life.

Chapter Thirteen

If Nina had let herself think about it, she'd have been paralyzed. As it was she had a job to do. She grabbed the portable radio the squad leader always wore from its holster around her waist and began firing orders into it.

"Beach emergency, all towers!" she barked. "Repeat—emergency, all towers. Do you read?"

There was a confused garble of responses as the towers reported back.

"Elizabeth, take the Jeep and pick up Wendy and Ben on your way. We're between Tower 3 and the South Tower. Jessica, get here as fast as you can. Everyone else, man your towers."

It was the best she could do, but Nina knew it wasn't enough. They had six people in the water and only five guards to rescue them—five guards who weren't even there yet. And meanwhile the Main Tower was unmanned. Throwing the radio

196

to Tom, Nina stripped off her shorts and raced toward the water without so much as a rescue buoy to help her. There was just no time.

Her arms sliced through the waves in strong, fast strokes, but Nina couldn't spot even one victim. *This isn't going to have a happy ending,* she thought grimly as she searched desperately for something, anything. She heard sirens on the beach behind her as the lifeguard Jeep arrived, maybe already too late.

Then suddenly, just in front of her, a head broke the surface, gasping frantically for air before it slid back under again. Nina immediately dove and began groping through the murky, storm-muddied water, trying to find an arm, a leg, some hair—anything she could tow the guy up by. She was almost out of breath when a strong, panicked hand closed tightly around her foot.

Adrenaline tinged with fear coursed through her like an electric shock. It was going to be a dangerous, nightmare rescue—the kind they made you practice in the pool. Nina knew very well that a rescuer never willingly let a panicked victim get a hold on her, but she also couldn't help thinking that at least she had the guy. She kicked furiously for the surface as the victim clawed his way up her legs. The guy outweighed her and he was terrified—he'd try to climb her like a ladder to get up to the air. Nina fought her own rising fear as she struggled to control him and get them both up to the surface.

"Stop it!" she ordered sharply as their heads broke into the sunlight and they both sucked desperately for air. "Let go of me and I'll help you."

But the drowning man was so afraid he didn't seem to hear her. He reached wildly for her neck, trying to pull himself onto her shoulders. Nina immediately ducked underwater to escape him. They'd taught everyone at lifesaving training that a drowning person would let go if you dove under, but this guy had obviously missed class that day. He held on in a stubborn, blind panic, his grip on Nina's throat tightening as they sank toward the bottom.

Stay calm, Nina told herself, feeling anything but. She placed her feet firmly against the victim's hips and pushed him away from her, at the same time forcing his arms upward with her hands and trying to duck her head out of his grip. It was exactly what she'd been taught to do, but it wasn't working—he was just too strong. They were entwined and sinking and Nina was running out of air. In the end she had no choice—she kicked him in the crotch. She'd learned that in lifesaving training too; you saved your own life first. The guy folded up like a rag doll and Nina turned him and grabbed him by the hair, kicking to reach the surface before he recovered. At last she broke into the air, gasping for breath while keeping her victim on his back in a tight, cross-chest carry.

"Just don't fight me," Nina begged in a low,

calm voice. "I promise I'll get you in." The guy moaned in reply, half out of it now, and she could smell the liquor on his breath as she began to tow him to shore.

"I've got this one." She heard a welcome voice behind her. It was Ben on the rescue board. Nina could have cried with relief.

"How long has he been unconscious?" Ben asked, sitting up on the board and reaching for a hand to pull the victim on with.

"He's not unconscious—I wish!" Nina could feel the salt stinging in the scratches all over her body. "He's probably got a pound of my flesh under his fingernails." She helped Ben maneuver the now docile victim into a prone position on the front of the board.

"I brought you a buoy." Ben shrugged the strap over his head and tossed it to her.

"Thanks." Nina's mind was racing. There were other victims yet to be rescued. "How many more people are still out here?" she asked.

"This guy makes three recovered," Ben said, lying on top of his charge in position to paddle. "But the one Wendy found is in pretty bad shape. The ambulance is on its way."

"Do you have any idea where the other three are?" Nina asked.

"We were all together," the guy on the rescue board slurred unexpectedly, speaking his first words. "We were right here."

"Take him in and send everyone out in this direction," Nina ordered Ben. "Hurry!"

Nina knew like she knew her own name that they had only six minutes. Six minutes before the brain started to die from lack of oxygen. Six precious minutes between life and death. She'd been in the water herself for at least five, and time had been lost on the beach before that. The only hope was that the other victims hadn't gone straight down—that they'd somehow managed to struggle and gasp long enough to save their own lives.

Elizabeth and Jessica sped through the water as Nina waved them toward her. "Start diving," she instructed. "Cover the bottom and pull up whatever you can grab."

But just then Jessica pointed beyond her. "I see one!" she yelled, streaking toward her target.

It was a girl, the hump of her bare back barely breaking the surface as she floated facedown in the swells. In seconds Jessica had flipped her over and placed her in a chin hold. Young and unconscious, the girl's pretty face was beginning to turn blue.

"Go, go, go!" Nina cried as Jessica kicked furiously for the shore.

Jessica passed Wendy on the way, and Nina, Wendy, and Elizabeth began to dive for victims. *Two more,* Nina told herself with every breath she took, with every beat of her heart. *Just two more.*

The water was only about ten feet deep where the boat had gone over, but it felt like a hundred.

Nina's lungs screamed in pain with every dive she took, and she knew she couldn't last much longer. She skimmed the murky bottom, her arms stretched blindly in front of her, praying to find the final two. If they had to bring out the scuba divers, Nina knew it would be to recover bodies, not victims. Suddenly her hands ran into something soft.

Her heart leapt—she'd found another one! Grabbing what felt like a handful of T-shirt, Nina kicked hard for the surface, her legs like lead. The victim seemed incredibly heavy as Nina dragged the lifeless form through the dark water. *Just a little farther,* she told herself, straining, exhausted, toward the light. *Just a little bit farther.*

"I've got one," she gasped, breaking the surface at last and pulling her victim's head up to breathe. It was a guy, completely unconscious and yet strangely peaceful looking. His expression stopped Nina cold.

"Give him to me," Ryan ordered, swimming to her side. "You're too tired."

"Ryan!" Nina exclaimed, only too glad to let him take over. At that moment Ryan's determined, capable face seemed like the most beautiful sight she'd ever seen. Nina struggled to flip her victim onto his back as Elizabeth and Wendy stroked to join the group.

They all saw it at the same time.

"Oh, wow. I can't believe it," Nina whispered, fighting tears.

The guy she'd just rescued held his girlfriend clasped tightly in his unconscious arms, her head tucked tenderly against his chest, her lifeless face as peaceful as his. Nina had found the final two.

"They could still make it," Ryan shouted as he split the victims and passed the girl to Elizabeth. "Let's move!"

Together the four guards streaked through the waves, reaching the sand in less than a minute.

Nina saw the ambulance approaching, saw Ryan and Elizabeth half carry, half drag their victims to dry sand, saw Ben and Jessica performing CPR on the girl Jessica had rescued, saw the other three victims puking up beer and salt water, saw the girl in the pink bikini crying with joy as she held their heaving heads, and at last she collapsed to her knees. She couldn't believe it—they had rescued all six. Three were very much alive, Jessica's victim was sputtering into consciousness, and even the last two had a chance.

"Come on, Nina." Wendy gently helped her back onto her feet and led her toward the others. "Don't you know you're a hero?"

"Again!" Jessica cried, her ear against the cold, clammy flesh of her victim's chest and her fingers on one lifeless wrist. There was no heartbeat, no pulse—nothing. She lifted her head as Ben applied renewed pressure over the girl's heart, attempting to mimic a heartbeat with short, rhythmic bursts of downward force. As soon as Ben had completed four strokes Jessica breathed hard into the victim's mouth, trying desperately to force air into lungs that were full of water. Ben immediately resumed his downward thrusts.

Jessica couldn't understand it—they were doing everything right. The girl's airway was clear and her head was tilted back to keep it that way, Ben was applying pressure to the heart in exactly the way they'd been taught, and Jessica was giving mouth-to-mouth for all she was worth. So why wasn't it working?

"Breathe!" Ben encouraged as Jessica put her mouth to the victim's again. "Breathe *hard!*"

Jessica breathed, watching out of one eye as the force of her breath lifted the victim's lifeless chest. They *had* to be doing it right. Ben knelt ready to push again as Jessica checked for a pulse.

"Wait!" She stopped him excitedly. "I think we've got her." She covered the victim's mouth with her own again, forcing another breath of warm air into the cold, resisting lungs. Then another. And another.

Suddenly Jessica felt the air rushing forcibly back out at her. She lifted her head just as the girl first coughed and then choked on the salt water that gushed from her mouth. Working quickly, Ben and Jessica turned the victim onto her side, keeping the airway clear as the girl vomited repeatedly onto the smooth wet sand. She was going to live.

"Wow," Jessica breathed quietly. She'd never experienced anything more intense in her life.

"You were awesome." Ben's voice was trembling.

Jessica's eyes locked with Ben's.

"You were awesome too," she said.

"What did *I* do?" he objected. "You found her, you brought her in, you did the mouth-to-mouth. I just helped a little."

"You helped a *lot*," Jessica corrected. "I couldn't have done it without you."

"I think you could have. You saved her life, Jessica."

Ben's intense blue eyes gazed deeply into hers and suddenly, unexpectedly, Jessica felt her own eyes filling with tears.

"Wait here for the paramedics," she told him, standing and rushing blindly down the beach toward her tower. She had to get away. From her victim, from the crowd, and—most of all—from Ben.

Nothing's changed, she thought bitterly as she ran, tears streaming down her face. *Right now he's impressed, but tomorrow he'll hate me again.*

And Jessica finally knew the truth. She didn't want Ben to hate her. She wanted him to love her. The way that she loved him.

Elizabeth watched transfixed from the edge of the water as the second ambulance sped off down the beach on its way back to the hospital. Everything had happened so quickly, and the odds had been so against them—it all felt like a miracle.

Jessica and Ben had already revived Jessica's victim by the time the first ambulance arrived, and the paramedics had revived the final two, the ones Nina had rescued from the bottom. It had been real horror-movie stuff for a while with the paramedics pulling out all the stops—Elizabeth shuddered at the recollection of the emergency tracheotomy they'd given the girl—but in the end they'd revived two living, breathing people. Not only that, the medics said that all six victims were going to be fine.

"Pretty hairy, huh?" Ryan said, joining her at the water's edge.

"The hairiest," Elizabeth agreed, shaken. She'd found one of the first three victims herself—a girl, still conscious. Wendy had rescued a guy who was too drunk and too full of water to fight much, but the belligerent, panicked guy Nina had rescued had almost drowned her. Elizabeth thought of the stupid fight she and Nina had had earlier in the afternoon and fought back tears. What if Nina had died?

"It's always bad when you find them unconscious," Ryan said, mistaking the source of her emotion. "You just never know."

Elizabeth thought she heard a catch in his voice, and she remembered the child who had drowned on Ryan's shift.

"Where were you today?" she asked hesitantly, not sure she was ready to hear the answer.

He shrugged and kicked at the sand. "Helping Captain Feehan. Some idiot stole the barge with all the fireworks on it, if you can believe that. I'd much rather have been on duty here. Thankfully, we were already on the way back when we heard Nina's emergency call."

"Someone stole the fireworks boat?" Elizabeth repeated, stunned. It seemed so trivial in comparison to what had just happened.

"Yeah," Ryan said. "Pretty stupid, huh? We finally found it in the estuary behind South Beach. Whoever took it really hid it well. I don't know why Feehan couldn't have used the Harbor Patrol to help him look, but he said I was in charge of the boat, so I had to find it. I felt like I couldn't . . . well, remember I told you I'm lucky to be on the squad at all this year. . . ." He let the sentence trail off, his meaning clear enough. He couldn't risk crossing Captain Feehan.

The tears overwhelmed Elizabeth before she even knew she was going to cry. Ryan took her into his arms as she sobbed with happiness and relief.

"I thought . . . I thought you'd run out on us," she managed through her tears.

"What!" It was clear from his voice that she'd hurt him deeply. "I thought you knew me a little better, Elizabeth."

206

Elizabeth realized her mistake at once. "It's just that people said . . . last year . . ." There was no good way to explain.

Ryan shook his head and tried to push her away, but Elizabeth held on.

"Don't be mad," she begged tearfully. "Please, Ryan. Don't be mad at me." Now that she had him in her arms, she never wanted to let him go again. All her resolutions to stay away from him evaporated like mist.

"I'm not mad," he said at last.

Elizabeth lifted her tear-streaked face hopefully to his. He didn't *look* mad—only sad and exhausted. Maybe they were meant to be together after all. Maybe . . .

"Ahem!" Tom's voice interrupted at her elbow.

Elizabeth froze mid-thought. She'd forgotten he was even on the beach. How much had he heard?

"Tom! Perfect timing, man," Ryan greeted him casually, handing off Elizabeth like a football. "Very big day, very scary rescue—your girlfriend needs you."

"Yeah, thanks," Tom said uncertainly, drawing Elizabeth into his dry, comforting arms. "Are you okay?" he asked her, genuinely concerned.

Elizabeth burst into tears again as she hid her face in her boyfriend's familiar SVU sweatshirt. The problem was, she didn't even know why she was crying anymore.

"Is she okay?" Tom asked Ryan anxiously.

"She's fine," Ryan assured him. "It happens. Look, I'll cover the Main Tower—why don't you take Elizabeth out and buy her a nice dinner?"

"I will." Tom held her tightly, protectively. "Thanks, Ryan."

The day had far exceeded Jessica's worst expectations.

"I can't *wait* to get out of here," she told Isabella as she stuffed armloads of unfolded clothes into suitcases, duffel bags, backpacks—anything she could find.

"Are you still sure you want to leave?" Isabella asked.

"Right after the fireworks," Jessica answered emphatically. "You promised!"

"All right," Isabella agreed, "but it seems like a shame."

"Why?" Jessica swept her makeup off the dresser and into an empty pillowcase. "You see how they all hate me."

"But that's just it, Jess," Isabella argued. "They don't. Wendy and Winston already apologized for the way they acted last night—they know it wasn't your fault. And Nina said you were incredible today. She's not mad."

"That's not everybody," Jessica sniffed.

"You have to admit that Elizabeth has a pretty good reason to be mad at you," Isabella countered.

"Maybe she does. So what? None of it matters now because I won't be here anyway."

Isabella groaned and lay back on Jessica's unmade bed. "You are so *stubborn*," she complained. "Why don't you admit this is all about Ben?"

"Ben!" Jessica scoffed, hoping she sounded convincing. "You must be kidding."

"I don't know why you hate him so much," Isabella continued unperturbed. "He seems pretty cute to me."

"Ben? *Cute?*" Jessica laughed, emptying her closet frantically. "I've certainly never noticed *that*."

But her laughter rang hollow, even to her. All she could see was the look of respect on Ben's face when she'd treated the guy with the bloody foot . . . the intense smile of triumph and accomplishment he'd flashed her when they'd saved a life together that same afternoon.

All she could see was the pain in his eyes when she'd said—no, *screamed*—that she hated him the night before. Tears burned her eyelids as Jessica bent to pack her shoes.

"I'm going home with you, Izzy," she said. "That's final."

Chapter Fourteen

"Ooooooh!" An indistinct but clear murmur floated up from the bonfires at the beach each time one of the massive skyrockets exploded overhead.

Elizabeth and Tom were standing a short distance from Isabella's packed car, watching the fireworks. Jessica was already inside, stubbornly insisting on leaving, and Danny and Isabella had wandered out to the yard to give Tom and Elizabeth some privacy.

An enormous red rocket exploded like a blossom, gold stars raining down from its center.

"Aaaaah," went the collective opinion.

"I'm so glad I got this chance to see you," Tom said huskily, pulling her close as the fireworks went off.

Ryan's fireworks, Elizabeth thought unhappily. *The ones he helped Captain Feehan recover. The ones he's shooting off on a barge out there this very minute.*

"Mmmm," she murmured, hoping Tom would take it for agreement.

"I've got to tell you, Liz," Tom continued, "when I saw you at the beach today—the way you handled that situation and saved those people's lives—I was so proud of you. I wanted to shout to anyone who'd listen that you were my girlfriend."

"Really?" she asked, touched.

He nodded. "I love you so much."

"Then kiss me," she said, bringing her lips to his.

They kissed—the slow, romantic kind of kisses that Elizabeth liked best. It was a storybook setting, and Elizabeth closed her eyes as their kisses gradually became deeper, hungrier.

Yes, she thought, opening her eyes dreamily to see the shimmering streamers in the sky, *this feels so right. What were we waiting for, Ryan?*

For a second she didn't even realize what she'd done, then she jerked her head backward. She was pretending Tom was Ryan! How could she stoop so low?

Unperturbed, Tom drew her lips gently back to his as more of Ryan's sparks showered the sky. It was clear he didn't have a clue there might be something wrong between them. "I'm not done with you yet," he whispered, kissing her again.

And I'm not done with you, she thought frantically, kissing him back. But his kisses did nothing for her now. Things with Tom just weren't the same—maybe they never would be again.

Maybe sometimes people drift apart without even realizing it, Elizabeth thought. *Maybe sometimes it takes someone new to wake them up.* Elizabeth didn't know, but one thing was clear—she needed to figure it out pretty soon.

"Will you miss me?" Tom asked as the fireworks finale began.

"Of course," Elizabeth said. Danny and Isabella were already walking toward the car, ready to leave, and Tom and Elizabeth moved to join them. "You know I will," she added, wishing she sounded more convincing.

"I'll miss you too." Tom reached for the car door handle. "In fact, I can't believe I'm saying this." He laughed. "But I almost wish it was September."

"Can we get this show on the road?" Jessica griped from underneath a mountain of luggage. Her complaint was answered by the sound of a revving motor as Isabella turned the key in the ignition.

"Bye," Tom said, brushing one last kiss across Elizabeth's cheek before he climbed into the car. "I love you."

"Bye," Elizabeth mumbled uncertainly.

She kept a smile plastered on her face until the taillights of Isabella's car were nothing more than two red pinpricks and the final, reverberating volley had dwindled into nothingness overhead. The tears welled up in her eyes.

What's wrong with me? she asked herself unhappily, gazing out at the blackening sea. *Tom came all this way to see me, and I wish he'd never come at all.*

"Oh, say does that star-spangled banner yet wave, o'er the land of the free . . . and the home of the brave?"

The applause from the concert audience was thunderous as Pedro belted out the final strains of the national anthem in time to the exploding skyrockets overhead. Wendy had never heard him sing so well or so powerfully—he was taking his listeners by storm. The fireworks finale ended with a series of earsplitting concussions and bright flashes, and Wendy twisted in her front-row seat to study the rapt faces packing the grassy amphitheater behind her. Many of them had come only because the concert was free, but no one there that night would ever forget the name Pedro Paloma, Wendy realized, tears of pride glistening in her full gray eyes.

The crowd gradually settled down as the echoes from the final explosion faded and Pedro held up his hand for silence.

"Thank you." Pedro smiled. "You know, 'The Star-Spangled Banner' was supposed to be our last song, but we have one more piece we'd like to do for you. Kind of a celebration, really." The people shouted their approval as Pedro held up his hand again, trying to speak.

213

Wendy was awed by the audience's reaction. *She'd* always known Pedro was a star, but she knew what she was seeing, too. His star was rising right before her eyes. This crowd couldn't get enough of him.

"If I could, I'd like to make a little announcement," Pedro managed to break in at last. "Me and the band here have some good news, you see. We've just been signed to do a six-city tour—opening for *Forced Entry!*"

The cheers in the crowds turned to screams as the mega-group's name was mentioned.

"Oh, you've heard of them," Pedro teased, grinning broadly.

Who hasn't? Wendy asked herself, stunned. Forced Entry was one of the biggest rock groups in the United States, maybe even the world. It was the chance Pedro had waited for for so long.

"We're leaving tomorrow for the rest of the summer," Pedro went on, "but before we go, I'd like to dedicate this one last song to the girl that I'll be missing while I'm gone—someone very, very special to me." He dropped his hand and the band launched into a cover of the old summer classic "Under the Boardwalk."

Wendy looked up into Pedro's face and smiled as he sang her his good-bye. She was so proud and happy for him—she wouldn't do anything to ruin this moment, Pedro's big break. He bent low from the stage to croon a suggestive line directly to her, and she forced herself to smile more brightly. When the song ended, Wendy was the first one on her feet, leading a standing ovation that seemed to go on forever.

You can cry later, she promised herself, cheering frantically with the crowd. *After he's gone, you can cry for the rest of the summer.*

"Mind if I join you?"

Nina's heart leapt. She'd climbed up onto the roof of the old Victorian on purpose to be alone, but the only person she was even remotely interested in talking to had just found her anyway.

"Hi, Paul," she said shyly, dropping her eyes from the shimmering display in the sky.

"Not mad at me anymore, I see," he observed, sitting down beside her on the bare gray shingles. The tennis shoes she'd abandoned in his boat the night before hit the roof beside him with a thud.

"Yeah, well, this morning when I heard you'd drifted all the way past South Beach before the Harbor Patrol towed you in, I pretty much had to believe your story," Nina admitted.

"Amazing," he teased, smiling.

"What's that supposed to mean?"

"Come on, Nina," Paul said. "I swear I don't know why, but most of the time you treat me like I'm a suspect or something. What is it about me exactly that makes you act so weird?"

"I don't act weird!" she protested, insulted.

215

"No?" he returned. "Jumping off a boat in the middle of the ocean at night isn't weird? And what about that tantrum you threw when I wanted to borrow your flags?"

"That wasn't a tantrum . . . ," she began, but trailed off in mid-sentence. There was no point arguing semantics—she knew what he meant.

Then, on the spur of the moment, Nina made a decision.

"You really want to know?" she asked suddenly, rushing ahead without waiting for his answer. "You *are* a suspect. Someone on the South Beach Squad is trying to sabotage us. How do I know it isn't you?"

"What!" he protested. "That's crazy."

"Is it?" Nina challenged. She ran through her evidence: the No Swimming sign, the poisoning of Paloma, the disappearance of the fireworks' barge that had kept Ryan off the job on the busiest day of the year.

"Wow," Paul said when she was finished. "Maybe you have a point. But I swear I don't know anything about a South Beach plot, and I *definitely* don't have anything to do with one. In fact, I probably saved Paloma's life. What makes you suspect me?"

Nina sat in silence a long moment, watching the fireworks light up the sky.

"You had a knife the day the sign was cut," she said at last. "And you found the dog first. You could have given him the hot dogs and then 'rescued' him to get me to trust you."

Paul looked genuinely shocked. For a moment Nina even thought he was going to get angry, but after a few deep breaths he managed a weak smile.

"It wasn't me," he said sincerely. "I'm hurt you could even think that." He took her chin gently in his hand and looked into her eyes. "Do you honestly believe I could do those things?"

"I . . . I don't know," Nina said. She was getting flustered again. He was just so incredibly handsome. "I guess not," she admitted.

"I'm glad." He smiled, leaning forward to kiss her.

"Paul!" she protested, planting her hands against his chest and turning her head in the nick of time. "I don't want to cheat on Bryan."

"Who's talking about cheating?" Paul asked. "Anyway, you two aren't engaged yet, are you? No one's signed on the dotted line?"

"No, but still—" Nina began.

"How much damage can one kiss do?" he interrupted.

"I don't know."

"Let's find out." Paul drew her into his arms.

Nina knew she should protest, but she didn't—she didn't want to anymore. She knew she loved Bryan, and the last thing she wanted was a summer fling, but Paul was here *now*, holding her *now*. The feelings she'd been fighting all summer overwhelmed her as she finally gave in and melted up against him, bringing her lips to his.

Overhead the fireworks finale sounded like World War III, but Nina barely heard it as she explored Paul's warm mouth, her hands buried in his short black hair. He was an incredible kisser, and the last bit of resistance left her body as they gradually fell back against the shingles, wrapped tightly in each other's arms.

"Wow!" she breathed as she pulled away at last.

"No kidding," Paul said, drawing her close again. "What do you say to an encore?"

Jessica figured it was probably two or even three in the morning. Every light in the beach house was off as she crept silently up the back walk from the alley, loaded down with luggage. The soft sea air smelled like a welcome home, and Jessica smiled with anticipation.

She'd had plenty of time to think about her reasons for leaving Sweet Valley Shore while Danny, Isabella, and Tom had chatted away on the long drive home. Jessica admitted to herself now that she'd made her decision in anger and stuck to it out of embarrassment. She dreaded facing her housemates and apologizing—especially to Ben—but she couldn't imagine the rest of the summer without them now, either. The most ironic thing of all was that Jessica had finally proved to them something she'd never even believed herself—she was an outstanding lifeguard.

Just a few miles from campus Jessica had given in. "Could you drop me off at the bus station, Izzy?" she'd asked quietly from the backseat.

"No problem," Isabella had answered, smiling her approval in the rearview mirror.

The bus ride back to the Sweet Valley Shore station had been slow and malodorous, but Jessica had barely noticed. A short taxi ride later she was back at the beach house, struggling with her bags. At last she deposited them on the back stoop and started digging through her purse for her keys.

A low, ominous growl sounded suddenly from the other side of the kitchen door.

Oh no, Jessica groaned silently. She hadn't counted on the dog being awake and in the kitchen.

"Paloma!" she whispered desperately through the wood of the door, searching for her keys more frantically. "Don't bark. It's only me—Jessica. Okay?"

The growling intensified.

"Stop it!" she hissed. "It's only me! The one who feeds you treats, remember?"

The growling stopped just as Jessica's hand finally encountered her keys. Relieved, she fumbled for the keyhole in the darkness and unlocked the doorknob.

The caterwauling half howl, half bark that Paloma unloosed as Jessica stepped into the kitchen was absolutely deafening. She'd never heard anything like it in her life.

"Paloma! No!" Jessica pleaded, holding out her hand for the dog to sniff.

But it was too late. Someone flipped a switch, and the kitchen was flooded with light.

"What the heck's going on here?" Ben demanded irately, his hands on his boxer-clad hips.

Chapter
Fifteen

"I'm sorry I woke you all up," Jessica began as Wendy finally stumbled in wearing an oversize blue T-shirt and fuzzy pink slippers. Everyone was there now, looking tired and washed out in the harsh, glaring light of the kitchen. They sat in the ladder-backed chairs around the wooden table: Wendy in her T-shirt, Winston in his sweat suit, Nina in a bathrobe, and Elizabeth in shorty teal pajamas.

Jessica's eyes skimmed her disheveled housemates as she tried to find a place to start. They were all looking at her expectantly, waiting to hear the reason they'd been summoned, and for a moment Jessica's courage faltered.

And then she saw Ben. Everyone else had grabbed chairs immediately, but Ben still stood stiffly by the counter, defiant in his boxer shorts. Jessica knew what she had to do.

"I think I owe you all an apology," she blurted before she could back out. "Wendy, I'm sorry about not watching Paloma Perro and the things that I said later. I hope you can forgive me."

"I already did!" Wendy protested. "I told you that wasn't your fault."

"Thanks," Jessica said. "And Winston, I know I was mean to you when you didn't have a job— walking around here like I thought I was some sort of queen or something. You must hate me."

"Don't be silly, Jess," Winston responded sincerely. "You *always* act like a queen. I barely even notice anymore!"

Jessica smiled in spite of herself as the rest of her housemates tried unsuccessfully to stifle their giggles. "Yes, well. Thanks, I think."

"Nina," Jessica continued, trying not to flinch as Nina lifted her dark head and looked directly at her. "I'm *really* sorry about everything I did to *you*. I mean, calling in sick . . . tricking you into taking my shifts. . . . It was totally irresponsible. I promise I'll never do it again."

Nina's face was stern, but a hint of a smile struggled with the corners of her mouth. "So you *admit* that you weren't actually sick," she pounced.

Jessica could feel the hot, embarrassed blush spreading across her cheeks as she averted her blue-green eyes. "Yes," she whispered. "I'm sorry."

"Apology accepted," Nina said warmly. "It's good to have you back on the squad."

"Thank you!" Jessica looked up again and her eyes met Elizabeth's.

"Liz," she faltered. "What can I say?"

"You tell me," Elizabeth said coolly.

Jessica looked uneasily around the room. This wasn't the perfect place to talk about Elizabeth's relationship with Ryan *or* the way Jessica had tried to torpedo it. Still, she had to say something.

"I just . . . it's just . . . you were right," Jessica stammered. "I mean, you were right about me and what I was doing. But that's all over now, okay? I'm taking myself out of the running."

Elizabeth raised her eyebrows suspiciously.

"I swear, Liz," Jessica begged. "Whatever you do is up to you, but either way I'm staying out of it. Can you forgive me? Please?"

Elizabeth stood and crossed the kitchen to within inches of her sister. "If you're lying . . . ," she began, her eyes boring into Jessica's.

"I'm not!" Jessica assured her. "I promise!"

Elizabeth held her gaze critically and then, miraculously, smiled—the warmest, friendliest smile Jessica had seen from her since the day they'd arrived at the beach house.

"I forgive you," Elizabeth whispered, wrapping her sister in a hug. "Welcome back."

Jessica was limp with relief as she returned Elizabeth's embrace, but she knew it wasn't over yet. She'd saved the worst for last.

"Ben," Jessica said, stepping back from

Elizabeth and squaring her shoulders. Gathering the remnants of her courage, she faced him where he stood on the other side of the kitchen. "I probably owe you the biggest apology of all."

Her voice quavered and she paused, feeling the tension in the room as everyone waited for her to continue.

"The other night . . . ," Jessica began, but her voice broke completely and she blinked back hot, sudden tears as she tried desperately to swallow past the lump in her throat. She drew in a shaky breath. "I've never said anything I've regretted more," she managed at last.

"It's okay." Ben stopped her, moving to stand at her side. "You don't have to apologize for that."

"But I want to," Jessica insisted, the tears overflowing and spilling disregarded down her cheeks. "I . . . I don't hate you," she whispered, her eyes fixed on his. "I never have."

"I know," he said. He took her gently into his arms and wiped away her tears with his fingers. "Come on—I'll help you with your suitcases."

It was four in the morning by the time everyone had gone back to bed and Jessica's luggage had been carried upstairs. Ben lingered just inside her door, the final backpack in his hands.

"Jessica?" he ventured as she threw her exhausted body onto her tiny single bed.

"Yeah?"

"I'm sorry too," Ben said. "I mean, I haven't exactly been a sweetheart myself. I've never seen anyone do anything as brave as you did when you faced us all tonight. Maybe I'm a genius, but I still can't figure out why you and I got off to such a bad start."

Jessica sat up and stared, surprised by Ben's apology. Suddenly his wrinkled old boxers could have been a tuxedo—he looked so handsome, he took her breath away. Her heart ached with wanting him.

"Who knows?" she answered, shrugging as her eyes raked regretfully over his tan, well-defined muscles. "Maybe it was destiny."

For a moment Ben seemed to freeze, reading her expression. Then he pounced. "I'll show you destiny," he promised huskily, dropping her backpack and bounding across the room.

In another second Jessica was in his arms, kissing him hungrily—kissing him with more emotion than she'd ever imagined she could experience again. She'd finally figured out she had feelings for Ben, but the sudden strength, the intensity of those feelings awed her.

"Ben," she whispered before he covered her mouth with more kisses.

"Don't say anything," he pleaded, his lips hot against hers. "Let me stay with you tonight."

"I don't know . . . ," she began.

"I love you, Jessica," he said, his arms tightening

around her protectively. "I've always loved you."

"I love you too," she murmured, surprised at how easy it was to say. Ben's eyes brimmed with emotional tears, and she felt her own fill in answer.

They were meant to be together—they were *going* to be together, Jessica realized as she clung to him. She couldn't believe she'd almost ruined everything by screaming that stupid, hurtful nonsense. Out of nowhere Madame Wolenska's turquoise eye shadow loomed up before her.

Jessica gasped.

"What?" Ben whispered. "Did I hurt you?"

"No," Jessica replied. "*I* hurt *you*." The fortune-teller had been talking about *Ben!*

It was barely past dawn, almost two hours before she had to be on duty, but Elizabeth hadn't been able to sleep after Jessica's reappearance. Not that she was sorry. The sun was already warm on her back, and Elizabeth smiled with anticipation as she crossed the remaining cool dry sand between herself and the Main Tower. It was a relief to know that Jessica wouldn't be chasing after Ryan anymore, and it was even more of a relief to have finally sorted out her own confused loyalties. After Tom's departure the night before, Elizabeth had come to a decision. She knew that Ryan cared for her, and she cared for him. That was all that mattered. This morning she was going to make him admit it no matter *what* she had to do.

"Hey, early bird," Elizabeth called cheerfully as she approached the tower and saw Ryan standing at the rail, a mug of coffee in his hand. He wore only his navy blue lifeguard sweats and a smile. Elizabeth thought he'd never looked so gorgeous.

"What are *you* doing here?" he asked, clearly surprised. "What time is it?"

"Don't panic. It's early." She laughed as she climbed the tower stairs and stripped off her jacket, exposing the red lifeguard suit underneath. "What's with the specs?" she asked, surprised to see him wearing wire-frame eyeglasses instead of his usual contact lenses.

"Excuse me!" he returned, still clearly confused by her unexpected appearance. "I haven't gotten around to putting in my contacts yet. In fact," he added significantly, "I haven't gotten around to doing *much*."

"Like what?" Elizabeth asked flirtatiously.

"The lenses, my trunks, my breakfast," he answered. "You know, the normal things we do before we're ready for work."

"Work doesn't start for over an hour," she said, taking off her sweatpants and stretching her toned, tan body beside him at the rail. There were a few early surfers in the water, but other than that the beach was deserted. "Besides, it looks like everyone had their fill of the ocean over the weekend," she added casually, trying to start a conversation.

But Ryan wasn't fooled. "You want to tell me why you're here?" he asked.

And suddenly she *did* want to tell him—more than anything.

"Ryan," she said, looking past the glasses and into his eyes, "I . . . I really care about you. Nothing's the same with Tom now. All I can think about is you."

"I already told—" Ryan began, but Elizabeth rushed over his words.

"And please don't tell me you can't be responsible for me or for someone getting hurt again, because you know what?" Elizabeth interrupted. "That's a cop-out. There's something between us and you know it."

"Elizabeth . . ."

"Just kiss me," she insisted. "Kiss me once and *then* tell me you don't want me."

He looked at her stonily, and for a minute she feared she had gone too far.

"That's what you want, then?" he asked without emotion. "You want me to kiss you?"

"Yes!" she exclaimed.

The next thing Elizabeth knew she was in Ryan's strong arms, exchanging deep, hungry kisses. It was even more electric than before, and she kissed him joyfully, with total abandon. It wasn't until the surfers started catcalling from the water that Elizabeth realized how publicly their pent-up, frustrated affection was on display.

"Let's move this into the tower," she suggested breathlessly and Ryan nodded his agreement, never letting go as he maneuvered her inside and shut the door behind them.

"Come here," he told her, sitting on the counter with his back to the glass and pulling her tightly to his chest. In a second Elizabeth was lost in his kisses again, forgetting Tom, forgetting herself, forgetting everything except how right it felt to finally be with Ryan. Their kisses turned teasing, experimental, then deep and passionate again. On impulse Elizabeth removed Ryan's glasses and tossed them onto the old vinyl sofa behind her, wanting nothing in between them. She leaned against him for support as her hands ran over his hard, muscular body. Somewhere in the back of her mind it occurred to her to wonder how much time had gone by, but she quickly dismissed the unwelcome thought. Time was frozen, suspended, unimportant.

"I should be getting ready," Ryan murmured, his lips soft against hers. "It's getting late."

"Just a few more minutes," she begged, clinging tightly. He stiffened momentarily, but then relaxed into her embrace, kissing her again and again as the time slipped by unheeded.

"Help! *Help!*"

The shriek from the beach cut through the glass walls of the tower like a knife. Ryan lurched up from the counter, practically pushing Elizabeth across the room. "My glasses!" he shouted desperately. "Where did you . . . ?"

But Elizabeth was already flying down the tower steps, a rescue buoy over her shoulder. She'd seen the broken surfboard the second she'd opened her eyes—and the unconscious boy still strapped to one useless half by his rubber ankle leash.

"Hurry!" the boy's surfing partner yelled as Elizabeth sped through the waves. "He's not breathing!" The other boy had turned his friend faceup and was trying to hold him above water in the pounding surf.

"I've got him!" Elizabeth shouted, loosing the unconscious boy from the broken tail of his board and grabbing him in a chin hold. She began swimming rapidly for the shore.

"He wiped out bad," the victim's panicked friend reported, paddling behind her. "He must have hit his head."

Elizabeth felt sand under her feet as she dragged the heavy body toward the shore. Ryan rushed into the white water to meet her, still wearing sweatpants. He'd found his glasses, but that was all he'd had time for, she realized.

"He's unconscious," Elizabeth reported as Ryan scooped up the boy and started running. "Possible head injury," she added a moment too late.

"Great!" Ryan exploded. He was already charging back toward dry sand with the boy draped across both arms, his head dangling wildly. "Anything else you want to tell me?" he snapped as he reached to support the injured kid's head.

And he *was* just a kid, Elizabeth realized as Ryan laid the unconscious boy gently on the sand and began mouth-to-mouth. He was probably no older than twelve.

"Damn!" Ryan yelled angrily. The boy still wasn't breathing. His young friend began to cry, great silent tears that ran down his cheeks unchecked.

"Call for an ambulance!" Ryan ordered. Elizabeth turned and fled.

She had barely signed off the radio when she heard the siren wail through the still morning air. Elizabeth grabbed blankets for the victim and his friend and ran back down the tower stairs, back to help Ryan.

"He's breathing!" she exclaimed excitedly, kneeling by the boy. He still looked out of it, but he was definitely breathing on his own.

"No thanks to you!" Ryan snapped rudely, snatching a blanket from her hands and wrapping it around the shuddering boy.

"What's that supposed to mean?" she asked, a sick feeling starting in the pit of her stomach.

"This is all your fault," Ryan accused in a hard, nasty voice. "I told you to stay away from me, but you think you know everything, don't you? Well, you want to know what? This kid almost died and *you* almost killed him!"

"What are you talking about? I *saved* him!" Elizabeth defended herself hotly, only too aware that the injured boy's friend was staring at them openmouthed.

"So you pulled him out of the water," Ryan spat. "So what? If he'd had a neck injury, you could have paralyzed him with a chin hold like that."

"What about you?" Elizabeth countered derisively. "At least I didn't run up the sand with him like a sack of potatoes! You think you're the only lifeguard on the beach with a clue what to do, don't you? Well, let me tell *you* something, Ryan Taylor—we all did just *fine* without you yesterday."

Ryan's face turned white with anger, and the veins in his neck stood out sharply. He might have said anything if the ambulance hadn't pulled up just then. Instead he turned his back on Elizabeth and began preparing the victim.

Elizabeth watched woodenly as Ryan and the paramedics transferred the wounded surfer into the ambulance and helped his shaken friend climb in beside him. The emergency vehicle was just pulling away when Nina and Wendy came sprinting across the sand, their faces concerned.

"What happened?" Nina asked Ryan.

Elizabeth waited for him to start shouting again, to humiliate her further, to tell everyone how it was all her fault for distracting him when he should have been working. But he didn't. Instead he handed his whistle wordlessly to Nina and stalked off down the beach, his back rigid and unapproachable.

"What was *that* all about?" Wendy wondered aloud.

Elizabeth burst into tears.

"Oh, hey," Wendy apologized quickly. "I'm sorry. What did I say?"

Nina put a comforting arm around Elizabeth's shoulders and drew her away toward the water. "Did you two have a fight?" she asked gently.

Elizabeth nodded, unable to answer. It just hurt so much. It was so unfair of him to blame that accident on her! And especially after what had taken place between them only minutes before, in the tower. . . .

"Some guys are impossible to understand," Nina soothed. "I'm afraid Ryan's one of them. You two will work it out."

But Elizabeth wasn't so sure. She could barely make out his silhouette now, far away down the beach. Was Ryan just walking, or was he walking out on them? Would he come back?

Did she even want him to?

Will Elizabeth get a second chance with Ryan Taylor or will his secrets keep them apart? Find out in Sweet Valley University #23, SWEET KISS OF SUMMER.

233